UTTERLY DECEIVED

Agatha van der Merwe

Malherbe Publishers Publication
Author: Agatha van der Merwe
Book cover: Malherbe Uitgewers

Set in Franklin Gothic Book 12pt
First Edition 2025

Copyright ©Agatha van der Merwe
ISBN 978-1-997443-01-8

1

It was a spectacularly beautiful morning in Mossel Bay, South Africa. The mist hovered low above the waves, giving it a mysterious, almost fictional, appearance.

Dwayne Foster and his sister, Lizelle Moore, were jogging along the beach as they usually did when he visited her and her husband, Henry. He enjoyed jogging with her casually, but to participate in races were not his forte as much as it was hers.

She glanced at him. Without reducing her pace she said, "May will most likely be discharged from hospital today."

"Yes, I know."

She hesitated for a brief moment, then spoke cautiously, "You know she will have to move in with you?"

"Have you gone insane?" he cried out, as expected, with great unease. "How do you think Bernice will respond to this outrageous idea of yours?" A frown appeared on his forehead. These past few days he was somewhat pre-occupied, lost in his own thoughts and he wasn't paying as much attention as he should have. Apparently, he did not keep up with all the developments.

She let out a sound similar to that of a single drop of water falling onto a brick, then responded dramatically, "I have no idea what you see in that woman! I do not like her one bit. Something about her is fishy, I tell you. One of these days she's going to disappoint you in one way or the other... Come to think of it, didn't she ask you to marry her, instead of waiting for you to do the proposing?"

He took great offence by her fiendish remarks and the tone in his voice was evidence thereof when he snapped back. "How my fiancée and I came to be, is none of your business!"

She came to a halt, standing motionless. She sounded rather confused. "Have you not told her about the situation with May already?"

"No."

She gasped, then closed her mouth and lifted her chin. "Oh well, she'll just have to accept that it is what it is, and there is nothing else that can be done about this."

"Please, remind me again why you and Henry cannot take her under your care for the time being?"

His annoyance reflected in his dark blue eyes. It even appeared as though his dark brown hair, ruffled by the wind with strands flying around in different directions, shared his mood.

"You know all too well that Henry and I will be leaving for America the day after tomorrow. How do you expect us to get someone who does not have a passport, or even an ID for that matter, an approved visa in one single day?"

A short, but intense silence ensued. He had totally forgotten about their flight leaving the day after tomorrow...

"There is no other way, Dwayne. Where else can she go?" She was clearly calm again as her voice was now soft and filled with sympathy.

He sighed. "Nowhere." He was starting to regret being the one who saved that helpless body floating along the shoreline a month ago. It was much more of a burden being a Good Samaritan, than it would have been to leave her there, pretending not to see her at all.

Instantaneously he felt guilty about his own selfish thoughts. "I'll pick her up as soon as we're done here."

May had been floating seemingly lifeless in the shallow waters of one of the beaches in Mossel Bay when he and Lizelle found her. If they had not decided to go jogging earlier than usual on that particular day, she would most definitely be in the cemetery right now, instead of the hospital. He was working on a new season for his quite popular TV-show: *Know your coastline – along the deep sea*, and the filming ended in Mossel Bay, three weeks after his twenty-seventh birthday. Consequently, he had a few days to visit his sister and her husband.

Finding May had completely ruined all of his plans as well as his schedule.

Lizelle encouraged, or rather forced, him to stay at May's side while she was in hospital. She argued that since he had been the one who saved her, he had some sort of obligation towards her now. If it wasn't for that, he wouldn't still be here.

May is not her real name either. He only called her May Neeman after no one came looking for her. No one seemed to know who she was before she was found afloat in the Indian Ocean. As such, he was also held responsible for paying the hospital bills. He had no problem with that, since he was certain she would compensate his expenses as soon as she regained consciousness and the required information could be acquired.

However.

May regained consciousness only a few days after she was admitted to hospital ... but she had absolutely no idea who she was, who her family was, where she came from, or how she ended up nearly drowning. And her memory had not returned yet.

When he found her in the water, he had assumed she was a tourist, because she was dressed in swimwear. He was quite certain that she had gone for an early morning swim and that a riptide had taken her to the depths, then spat her out after she lost consciousness – like it would spit out a dead, half eaten seal. Only people unfamiliar with the ocean would do such a senseless thing, was the thought that roamed his mind.

He was convinced he could jog her memory by telling her his theory on how he believed she landed in the ocean. She listened with great attention, thought about it for a couple of moments and then told him that she honestly had no idea if she had been on vacation or not, or whether she lived in Mossel Bay or somewhere else. She did not even remember going swimming that morning.

Initially he did not mind her amnesia. As time went by though, the truth dawned on him like soft rain on an over-packed backpack on a hiking trip. A month had passed since she was rescued, but there was absolutely no progress – she still did not remember anything ... The only people she knew now, were him and Lizelle, because they were the only ones who visited her in hospital.

* * * * * * * * *

"So, *this* is the mermaid you've acquired yourself, mate. It is very nice to meet you, mermaid May," Pedro Oliver said in a playful tone when Dwayne and May walked into Dwayne's house in Hermanus later that day. Dwayne had contacted him earlier and asked if he would please come over to his house in advance and prepare the guest room for her. He had never visited the woman Dwayne had saved in hospital, purely because he did not think they would ever meet. He thought she would return to her home the moment she was discharged.

The way Pedro looked at her, made her feel nervous.

"Hey," she replied shyly.

He laughed, then turned his eyes towards Dwayne. "What were you thinking calling her May, mate? She looks nothing like a May." With a smile around his lips, he turned his eyes back towards her. "We'll have to think of a more appropriate name. Perhaps Blondie, Little Nymph, Bella ... what do you think?"

"There is nothing wrong with the name Dwayne gave me," she said with self-consciousness noticeable in both her voice and body language.

It was Pedro's nature to tease everyone about everything, and usually Dwayne found it amusing too, but today, for some unexplained reason, Pedro's jokes upset him. "Don't be silly! ... May, he's trying to be funny. Ignore him."

If only he knew how embarrassed she was as she did not like to be the center of attention at all. She could not help but wonder for a brief second if perhaps *that* was one of her personality traits before she forgot everything. To hide her unease, she offered to go and make coffee or bring anything they wanted to drink – even though she had no idea where anything was in Dwayne's kitchen. She told herself that searching through the cupboards would give her some alone time, and besides, by doing this she would acquaint herself with the layout of the kitchen too.

She had no idea why she felt so uncomfortable in their presence. Her heart pounded against her ribcage and she spent an extensive period of time in the kitchen – completely unnecessarily, because she had found everything rather fast.

"Listen man, we cannot put off filming any longer," Pedro said as soon as May had left the lounge. "You'll have to bring your mermaid with. If we don't start filming tomorrow, we'll never be done on time."

His naughty smile when he used the word 'mermaid' put Dwayne on edge. "I know we cannot postpone any longer, Pedro, but there is not enough space on my yacht to accommodate her too."

"Nonsense. There is more than enough space for all of us." Pedro, on the other hand, made it sound as if Dwayne's yacht was the size of a cruise ship. He was, however, more accurate in his concept of the space on the yacht than Dwayne. He also knew Dwayne was not really concerned about space. Something else was bothering him.

He ran his fingers through his light-brown curly hair and the expression in his green eyes changed. "Have you contacted the police yet? Clearly no one reads the papers anymore, mate."

"I was really hoping it wouldn't come to that. I truly thought that by now she would have regained her memory and be off to her home. Or that someone would have responded to the article placed in the paper or any of the posts on social media at least. As you said, we need to start filming tomorrow. So, I'll go to the police when we get back. They'll probably recommend she stays with me until they manage to find her family anyway, or until further notice." He did not want the drama of a police investigation hindering the filming of their show, but getting the police involved was inevitable. Nevertheless, he was determined to get through filming in peace first, then he would contact them.

"You know there is someone who can help you with this particular ... situation?"

Dwayne leaned forward. "I have already called Terry. He said that without at least a name there is nothing he can do. Even the name of a relative or a spouse if she's married, or a surname or an address, anything. But I have absolutely nothing to give him."

"So, you are now stuck with her until the police somehow manage to achieve some miracle?" Pedro by now had totally forgotten to mind how loudly he was speaking.

"Yes, she is my problem for now!" He turned his head into the direction of the door where May entered. From the look on her face, he immediately deduced that she had heard everything. He got up to take the tray from her, but she turned her back on him, facing Pedro.

Pedro quickly poured milk and sugar into his mug, then removed it from the tray, and while she did not say a word, from her gaze he could see she was upset. He realized too late (as always) that he had totally forgotten to regulate his volume and to filter his words.

She put the tray on the table in the middle of the living room and rushed out.

Dwayne felt tremendously guilty as he watched her disappear through the door.

They drank their coffee in silence. No one dared utter a word. As soon as the mugs were empty, Pedro greeted his friend and left. He almost got the impression Dwayne blamed *him* for upsetting May – and maybe it was his fault. Had he not discussed the matter with Dwayne right away, she would not have overheard the conversation. If only he had waited!

Dwayne set out to find May, embarrassed about the conversation he and Pedro had, but there was nothing he could do to change that now. He found her lying on the bed in the guest room. Luckily, he had told her which room would be hers while they were travelling home from hospital earlier. He noticed yet again how picture-perfect her light blue eyes matched her golden blonde hair, and how it created an illusion of fragility.

Softly her shivering voice filled just enough space for him to hear when she spoke. "I'm sorry I have become a burden to you. I hate being a burden, especially to you. You have done so much for me already. If you want to send me off to someone else,

I will not object. I know you will leave me in good caring hands. Oh, how I wish I could get my memory back so I can return to my own home." Her eyes teared up.

As if pushed by instinct, he took a step forward, instantly feeling sorry for her. How hard must it be to have no idea who you were.

"No, May, I didn't mean it like that. You are not a burden. The thing is, I must be off tomorrow to start filming for my TV-show... and I don't know if you would be able to manage spending a week on the ocean in a yacht with me ... us. And I don't know what to do if you don't want to come along. Will you join us?" He certainly hoped that the idea of spending a week on a yacht on the open water with a bunch of strangers, didn't give her an overwhelming feeling of anxiety and fear. After all, it was in the ocean where she had almost died.

"If I won't be in your way, I'd like to go with you." She would much rather be terrified on the ocean with him, than alone on solid soil with strangers. He had come to accept and respect the fact that she would probably never regain her memory, but she was afraid no one else would do her that courtesy.

He smiled, relieved. "You will not be in our way, thank you, May."

2

Early morning, as the sun seemed to shine from the bright golden water rather than itself where it barely cleared the horizon, they observed the white-and-turquoise, forty-five-foot yacht entering the harbor in Cape Town with great admiration.

Dwayne had appointed Shane as Skipper, since he preferred to dive and do the filming of the underwater scenes himself, together with Pedro. Shane and Thomas were the only other crew members besides him and Pedro.

Thomas threw the rope out and quickly secured the yacht to the docks.

There was an electric atmosphere of excitement. The next season of their show was going to start off in Cape Town.

This is the life, Dwayne thought to himself, as icy cold adrenaline surged through his veins in anticipation.

Just as May was about to board, she stopped in her tracks in a state of panic. Flooded with fear, she wanted to run away as far and as fast as possible, but she could not move. "I cannot board that!"

Dwayne jerked his head around. "Why not?" He frowned, totally confused by her sudden terror. She had seemed fine and actually excited to board only a few seconds ago.

"I can't. I can physically not move, can't you see?" she called out like an innocent accused of treason, who suddenly realized she was about to be placed on the chopping block. Her heart was in her throat. She had no idea why she was so afraid all of a sudden, because it was a beautiful day, the ocean calm and clear. She could even see the fish swimming in the dock.

He gaped at her. Then it hit him that it was possibly her body and mind protesting since she had so nearly drowned merely a month ago.

Before he could react, Pedro placed his hand gently on her shoulder and said, "Don't worry, my little nymph, it's understandable that you would be afraid. But I can assure you, this is the safest vessel you will ever set foot on. Come, let me help you. I will not let you touch the water. While we are sailing, I will take it upon myself to ensure you stay on board the entire time … and when I'm diving, I'll appoint Shane to look after you."

Her heart beat at a speed not healthy for any human being, as she tried to convince herself there was nowhere else to go. It was going to be fine; she should get over her fear and board the yacht. She took a deep breath, then nodded at Pedro, giving him permission to help her board.

Dwayne pursed his lips, not pleased at all. What made Pedro think that he would not personally protect her while they were on the ocean? Or that he would not ask Shane or Thomas to look after her while they were busy filming?

* * * * * * * * * *

Later that evening Dwayne and May sat in the owner's cabin and reviewed the quality of the edited footage of what would become the first episode of the new season. The yacht swayed rhythmically with the waves, creating a general feeling of tranquility.

"You are a natural, May," he said, pointing at the screen of his laptop.

"Only because you taught me exactly what to do."

"I only showed you once, and it's not that easy or straight forward. You are a fast learner."

"Thanks, Dwayne. These underwater scenes are simply breathtaking! It must be an amazing experience to see it with your own eyes?"

She clearly appreciated the beauty in the footage of his and Pedro's first dive.

"It's an experience one can never get used to. Did you know that coral reefs are referred to as the rainforest of the ocean?"

"No, I did not know. Why is it called that?"

"Because it is one of the most diverse and richest eco systems on earth. Coral reefs cover less than zero-point-one percent of the ocean's floor, but serves as a home to more than twenty-five percent of all marine life." He could not hide his excitement; but then again, he was not trying to.

"Wow, that is impressive."

A smile formed around his lips and a short comfortable silence fell between them.

Then she said, barely louder than her thoughts, "I think I would have loved to do deep sea diving, if I hadn't been so terribly afraid of water, of course."

He considered his words carefully before responding. "Perhaps one day you will conquer this fear and then you can learn."

"Who is Pedro?" A drastic change in topic, she knew, but she did it on purpose, since the alternative would be to reply on his remark ... and she was convinced she would never overcome her fear of water. Defeating death once, was lucky, doing something dangerous like deep sea diving would be tempting fate.

"Pedro is my partner and co-host of *Know your coastline – along the deep sea*," he answered with a frown between his eyes. He had already told her everything she needed to know about Pedro. He could not help but wonder if her short-term memory was also starting to deteriorate now. She did not have a problem remembering anything that happened or what they talked about since she regained her consciousness in hospital up until now.

She smiled faintly, relieved that she was no longer the center of attention. "Why did you choose that specific topic and title for your show?"

"South Africa is flooded with television programs about the wildlife, mountains, the desert roads and culture. There are only a few TV-shows about the incredibly diverse and interesting ocean life and shipwrecks off our coastline. People are unaware of the amazing treasures lurking a stone's throw away. We wanted to show that to our viewers, take them on a journey all along the deep sea." His eyes sparkled. It was obvious that this was his passion.

"That's brilliant," she said smiling.

Pedro entered and interrupted their conversation. "Are you done here, little nymph?"

"My name is May. Please stop calling me little nymph or mermaid."

He only laughed. "Come, look at the stars, it's breathtaking."

Dwayne got up. "The night sky is quite remarkable out here, you should definitely see it, May. Let's go."

She followed them outside.

"Wow, this is truly indescribable," she said, unable to move her eyes from the heavens.

"Isn't it?" A smile touched Dwayne's lips.

"Thank you for showing me. I have never seen anything like this!" Or at least, nothing she could recall.

"Of course," Pedro responded quickly. "I thought you might appreciate it."

"I do."

They spent quite a bit of time on the deck, admiring the night sounds of the ocean. The intense darkness, due to the lack of moonlight, spurred the stars into shining even brighter, changing the normally awe-inspiring view into something spectacular.

* * * * * * * * * *

The days flew by, especially since May kept herself busy with the editing of each day's footage.

Her fear that she might somehow finish her final act that was interrupted, faded as time went by. Occasionally, she relaxed completely. Some days she did not even think about the water surrounding them at all. Though, even in her state of relaxation, no memories made their appearance.

In the blink of an eye, the week came to an end.

She, Dwayne and Pedro sat in the owner's cabin, each with a drink in their hands to enjoy the last few hours on the ocean while they headed back to the harbor.

She stared out of the window. Her eyes met the horizon. If only she could remember something. Anything – no matter what.

"Where is our mermaid dwelling so lost in thought?" Pedro's playful voice ripped her back to reality. "Thinking of the good old days, swimming and stealing sailors from their pirate ships, dragging them to the depths? Although, it probably was not that great, because in those days you hadn't met us yet." He'd been watching her for quite a while and had noticed how her facial expressions changed with her thoughts.

It was quite difficult to get used to his eccentric personality, but she finally managed to. Last night, she also made the decision that she would no longer try and get him to stop calling her mermaid or little nymph. He had not paid attention to any of her previous appeals anyway.

She looked at him with eyes shaded in sadness. "I was wondering why I can't remember anything. How can one's brain simply decide to lock up your memory and deny itself access to it? Did I even exist before a month ago, Pedro?"

When Dwayne had told him a couple of weeks ago about her condition, Pedro's first reaction was that it was impossible to forget everything about yourself. He was very skeptical and suspicious about this so-called total memory loss... However, the week he had spent with her on the yacht had given him new insight and changed his mind.

"May, you will see, not too long from now those precious memories will find their way back," he said without the usual teasing tone in his voice.

"And what if that never happens?" Tears filled her eyes.

"Then it doesn't matter anyway. What matters, is that you are alive. That you are not alone, you have me and Dwayne." It was a fruitless attempt to put her nerves at ease.

"No, I don't."

A frown appeared between Dwayne's eyes. "Why would you say that?"

"Because you have your own lives, with your own family and friends. Family and friends whom I am not a part of."

Dwayne tilted his head slightly and narrowed his eyes for a brief moment, wondering what triggered her to feel so absolutely hopeless. His own thoughts about the situation were constantly jumping back and forth, naturally, but he would not back down from his responsibility towards her.

"That is where you are making your first mistake, May. You are a part of our lives now, whether you like it or not."

"This is not about what I like or don't like, Dwayne, this is about you, I cannot expect you to..."

"And this is not about us either. You are already part of our lives. Our friends and family will accept you unconditionally the way you are, just like we did."

"Even if I never regain my memory?" she whispered almost inaudibly.

"Even then," he replied in a soft voice too, but his eyes pierced hers with an expression of finality and certainty – sending the message that he was done discussing the subject.

As they approached the harbor, the trio went and stood on the front deck. They stared at the docks as if, if they were to look away, they would disappear.

"What a great week this has been. Thank you." Dwayne was the first to break the silence. Within him he was dancing with joy for the incredible footage they had captured but he also felt sorrow because the week had come to an end.

"I see great success in the immediate future of this season, mate," Pedro responded, also pleased with what they had achieved.

May smiled. She glanced at Pedro and then looked at Dwayne. "Thank you both so much, I've learned more than I could ever have hoped for. Plus, I had fun."

Standing on the docks was a woman, waving at them, smiling.

Dwayne responded with a smile and waved back at her.

Without too much interest, May turned her eyes towards the woman who had clearly caught Dwayne's attention. Her heart almost stopped beating immediately. "No!! What is Bernice doing here?!"

A memory surfaced without warning and played in her mind like a film: *She is being pushed around by three people, quite brutally and violently – two unrecognizable men and Bernice. She's on a yacht and wearing swimwear, but not of her own accord. Now they are tying her up, attaching weights to her body. She's struggling and kicking to no avail. This only hurts her already injured body even more. They lift her up, in perfect unison, smiling. All yelling insults at her at once, laughing ... Splash!*

As the water flooded her memory, terror flooded her body.

Leaning closer, Dwayne whispered a response, loaded with more questions than it answered. "She is my fiancée." An intense frown divided his usually flat forehead into two very distinct halves. How on earth did she know Bernice, and how in this universe could she remember her?

She jerked her head towards Dwayne and glared into his eyes. "Have you come to rectify what you failed at last time?" She struggled to breathe. If he was indeed Bernice's fiancé, then surely, he was one of the two men who helped to throw *her* overboard. And Pedro? Was he in on it too? Was he the other man? Those thoughts eased none of her fears, in fact, it turned them into horror.

Dwayne and Pedro's jaws dropped simultaneously as they gawked at her, then at each other.

She almost tripped when she rapidly darted towards the owner's cabin; in case Bernice could see her too, or worse, they all decided to corner her. She slammed the door shut, as though it would provide an extra layer of protection. Her body shivered uncontrollably.

"Turn around, Shane. Now! Tell them we cannot dock safely because something is wrong with the steering, tell them anything you want to! Just buy us some time." Dwayne shouted orders frantically to the Skipper while he headed to his cabin as well, Pedro short on his heels.

He tried to open the door, but she had locked it from the inside. "May! What's going on? Open the door, please."

"Go away!" she replied.

He turned towards Pedro. "Go and get my extra set of keys from Shane. Now! Hurry!"

"Okay," he ran back, up the stairs.

Dwayne's heart was in his throat, he was even more confused than a few seconds ago when he learned she knew Bernice. "Please, open the door. Let's talk about this."

No response.

"Here, mate." Pedro handed the set of keys to Dwayne. He was out of breath, he could not remember when last he ran that fast.

"Thanks." Dwayne searched for the right one, then inserted it quickly and somewhat shakily into the lock. Turned. When he pushed the door to open it, May instantly sat down against it, putting all of her weight into keeping it closed.

"Don't make me force this door open!" He glanced at Pedro and whispered, "She's blocking the door herself. Help me open this."

Pedro nodded.

On the count of three they charged, shoulders first, barging the door open and tumbling into the room as it flew open effortlessly.

She had since moved away from the door and was standing as far away from them as she possibly could.

The moment Dwayne regained his balance; he grabbed her by the arm. "What is going on here?"

"It was you, wasn't it? You and Pedro! You tried to kill me, together with that woman!" She ripped her arm free from his firm grip. She was drowning in fear and anxiety, and her fight or flight impulse was working overtime. "You lied to me! You made me believe that I could trust you! You were there on that day, with her, beating me up. I did not almost drown because I went for a swim, like you claimed! I almost drowned because you *threw* me into the ocean to drown. Why did you want to kill me, Dwayne? Why?" She was now sobbing uncontrollably, hitting him on the chest as hard as she could with both fists.

"May!" His voice echoed like thunder crashing through the room, bringing even the waves to silence. "What are you talking about?"

Pedro moved in behind her, took her by the wrists, and folded her arms across her chest.

"Please, don't throw me into the ocean again. I'm begging you." She struggled to get loose from his grip; but he held onto her wrists even tighter. "Please, don't listen to her again. If you have to kill me, do it first, before you leave me to the sharks, and please, don't tie weights onto me again."

Dwayne's heart was racing faster than his feet would, had he been sprinting. "That's ridicules! We did nothing of this sort." It was too much for him to handle anymore and he stormed out. Furious. How dared she accuse them of attempted murder, out of the blue like that, with no explanation whatsoever?

They could not waste any more time, it would only arouse suspicion if they delayed any longer. When they were finally ready to disembark, Dwayne told Shane to ensure May did not leave his cabin until he and Bernice had left. "Do whatever it takes," he commanded.

"Of course." He was prepared to do whatever it took to prevent her from leaving. He was well aware of what was happening, he did after all witness her reaction when she recognized Bernice.

May wept; her strength left her body and her knees started shaking.

Pedro kept her upright, then turned her around and looked her in the eye. He pulled her closer for a hug of sympathy. He was stunned by the sudden turn of events. Speechless. Without even realizing it, his thoughts became words, "Is that what happened that day? You were attacked, and when you saw Bernice, it triggered a memory? A memory you somehow connect to us?"

She did not respond, but kept on struggling to free herself from his grip until he eventually let her go. She had managed to pull herself together in some way, and she gave a few steps backwards.

A very strange feeling came over him, and for a brief moment he wondered how much of this new 'memory' was true and what was fabricated and clouded by her emotions.

"Seeing that you have regained your memory, would you mind telling me your name?"

"I don't know my name," she replied rather strongly, but something within her was beginning to long for death.

He shook his head, "You know, if you were attacked like you said, Dwayne and I had nothing to do with it. We had never even seen you until he found you floating out there." With his index finger, he pointed to the window overlooking the stretch of ocean. He wanted to say that Bernice had nothing to do with it too, but he could not speak for her, because he barely knew her.

She glared into his eyes with great confusion, anger and hopelessness.

The door flew open and Shane entered. He gaped at May for a few seconds, then turned his eyes towards Pedro. "They are gone. It's safe to come out now."

Dwayne's entire body shivered from shock and anger when he reached Bernice. He quickly greeted and was about to express how glad he was to see her, when she interjected, "Who's that woman who was standing next to you on your yacht?"

"Her name is May Neeman. She and Pedro have been together for about two months now. He invited her to join us on the trip." It took everything in him to sound steady and calm. He could not explain why he suddenly assumed that if what May had said about Bernice was remotely true, he would endanger her life by being honest. He did not believe a word of it himself. But IF there were any truth in May's story whatsoever, and Bernice were to believe that she was simply Pedro's girlfriend, she would not suspect her of being her death's escapee. Not that he believed Bernice had anything to do with it for one second, but … This entire situation was a chaotic mess and he was not certain how to handle it at all.

"Oh, thank goodness, she almost looked like…" She stopped talking and bit on her lower lip.

Being calm and in control, were becoming nearly impossible for the man approaching the edge at lightning speed. Suspicion and even more confusion overwhelmed him the instant he learned that she had recognized May, but that she was actually relieved to hear she was someone else.

"Who did she look like, Bernice?"

"An old school friend with whom I lost contact about five years ago."

She appeared indifferent, but the nervousness in her voice did not escape him.

"Does this old friend of yours have a name?" He tried to replace the hurricane inside his stomach with an illusion of curiosity.

"What's it to you what her name is?"

"Why are you avoiding my question, are you hiding something? You know how angry it makes me when you don't answer simple straightforward questions!"

Startled by his sudden outburst, she moved her shoulders slightly. Never in the past had he ever raised his voice to her. "Her name is Vanessa Vincent. Happy?"

"Yes." Then he sighed. "I am sorry I yelled at you. It was a long, difficult week and I am tired, but it didn't give me the right to take it out on you."

"It's fine."

"I'll make it up to you when we get to my house."

"I'm not going to your house, Dwayne. I have only come to see you quickly. My flight leaves in an hour and a half. I have to get back to the airport now."

"So soon? Why?"

"I have to be back at work tomorrow morning."

"Very well, then. I'll take you to the airport, it will give us a little bit of time to be together at least. Let's go."

"No, it's not necessary. I rented a car to come here, so I have to take it back to the airport. Don't follow me. Go home, you are tired."

He pursed his lips, narrowed his eyes and glared at her for a moment in silence. "All right, I'll leave.

Have a safe flight. Please, let me know when you are back home." He turned around and walked away without looking back at her again. He was angry. Totally confused. He even felt rejected.

His mind was in complete disarray while he headed for Pedro's house. What if May was telling the truth, and Bernice had really tried to kill her? His heart contracted with pain. No, that was impossible. Bernice was probably the one telling it as it truly was. They were only old school friends who had last seen each other five years ago ... and most likely, that's the reason why May recognized and remembered her. Perhaps she got confused as to how and where Bernice fitted into her past. Bernice was after all his fiancée; he should take her word over that of someone he barely knew. He should give her the benefit of the doubt, even if she was clearly not pleased to have seen May on his yacht. But, on the other hand, May was so frightened and scared when she saw Bernice, it was almost impossible not to take her seriously. All he knew, was that he needed to get to the bottom of it. Fast!

"She is finally asleep," Pedro said, as if reporting on a patient to her doctor, when Dwayne entered.

"Thanks, Pedro. Has she said or remembered anything else?"

"No, apparently she doesn't remember anything else, not even her own name. I asked her but she had nothing to add. She was completely in shock, mate. She struggled to calm down. She was emotionally drained by the time we had her room ready, so I gave her a natural sedative to take the edge off. Initially she didn't want to take it, but I convinced her I meant her no harm, she would be safe."

Dwayne had not asked him earlier to bring her here, he instinctively knew that that was what his friend wanted him to do. He assumed that since Bernice was going with Dwayne to his house, it would be best for May to be here until Bernice was gone again.

A short silence ensued.

"What do you make of all this, mate?" Pedro posed the question as carefully as he could.

"I don't know, but I fully intend to get to the bottom of this, as soon as humanly possible. ... I think I might have found out her real name." He believed it to be her name; not only because Bernice had said so, but because May recognized and remembered Bernice first.

"How on earth did you find that out?"

"Bernice told m.."

"Bernice? But ... how? Did you discuss May with her?"

"Of course not."

"Then ... then she must have seen her on the yacht and recognized her too?"

"Yes. She said that May looked like an old school friend, Vanessa Vincent. On my way here, I called Terry and asked him to investigate, but we'll have to wait for his confirmation before we can be sure."

"Where is Bernice now? Where did you tell her you were going? What did you tell her about May?"

"I didn't have to tell her anything, because she left only minutes after we docked. She said that she needed to be back at work in Durban tomorrow, she only came to see me quickly." He was quite suspicious about the fact that she was so eager to leave so hastily, shortly after his arrival, but he kept his thoughts to himself. "I told her May have been your girlfriend for the past two month already."

"Why?"

"Because I didn't want to put May in danger unnecessarily."

"Do you actually think Bernice has ..."

"No! Of course not."

Pedro's eyebrows raised. "Well, speaking of Durban, you remember your meeting with Marcell, the head of nature conservation? That's three days from now."

"Of course, yes."

"What about May?"

"I'll have to take her with me."

"Really? Where is she going to stay when you are attending the meeting? And where is she going to stay when you visit Bernice? You said earlier that you plan on visiting her after the meeting. What do you think will happen if you bring them together? Do you really think May can handle that?"

"No, you're right. That is a stupid idea. I'll have to think of another plan." The entire business with May had unexpectedly escalated into something he was not prepared for. "Can she stay here with you while I am away?"

"Of course she can."

"Thanks."

He spent another half an hour at Pedro's house, in case May woke up. When it became clear that her sleep was deemed to last until morning, he got ready to leave. "I'll come and get her tomorrow morning and bring her back when I leave for Durban."

On his way home, his thoughts drifted. He had met Bernice O'Brian two years ago when he and Pedro spent the weekend at the school where she was teaching. The school was hosting an event to which they and a couple of other TV-presenters were invited. It was a charity event, the school was hosting a fundraiser, and afterwards donated a substantial amount of money to the Retirement Home in the community.

Bernice was responsible for him and Pedro. She had to book their accommodation and see to it that they received their food and drink on time. She had to ensure that their equipment was set up without damage before the presentations, and that it was stored safely afterwards.

He took her number when the weekend came to an end and made an effort to stay in touch. He never missed the opportunity to visit her when he went in the general direction of Durban. She came to visit him in Hermanus three times, and he invited Lizelle and Henry too so they could meet her. From the start Lizelle and Henry disliked her. He did not care though, and his friendship with Bernice became more intimate as time passed. It was clear to him that she loved her learners, and found great joy in their energy and enthusiasm. Her passion for her work was obvious and because his work was his passion too, they connected instantly.

One morning she called him and asked whether he did not think they complemented each other perfectly. He said he absolutely agreed. Her marriage proposal followed automatically and he said he could not see any reason why they should not get married.

However, after their engagement, her work suddenly demanded all of her time. They barely talked anymore; and when they happened to see each other, it was rarely for longer than an hour.

* * * * * * * * * *

Just around the corner from where she left Dwayne at the harbor, Bernice started to search desperately in her purse for her cell phone – the one Dwayne did not know about.

"Oh, come on! Where are you?" she called out in frustration since she could not find it fast enough for her liking. Finally, she got hold of it and made the call to her superior, John Hall.

The call went through and she immediately shouted, "I just saw someone who looks exactly like Vanessa!" She didn't even give him the opportunity to greet properly.

His response was calm, in contrast with her hysterical speaking. "Would you calm down, Bernice."

He waited a few seconds for her to get her emotions under control, then continued, "You are going to see her in every crowd you look. Her face will be everywhere until you come to peace with the fact that she is truly dead. That is the way these things work. She will haunt you until you are comfortable again that she poses no threat to you any longer."

"How can you be so convinced that she actually died? That woman was real, and she looked exactly, and I mean exactly, like Vanessa! What if it really was her, John?" She was loaded with anxiety and shock from seeing Vanessa alive and well on Dwayne's yacht. She had no idea how it was possible that Vanessa could have survived the ordeal. Dwayne had told her that that woman's name was actually May and that she had been in a relationship with Pedro for more than two months already, but it did not ease her anxiety. She had to confirm with John.

"Vanessa is dead, Bernice. Get it in that thick skull of yours, okay?"

Only silence followed his remark.

"There is no way she could have wriggled free from those weights in her condition. Even if by some miracle she did, there is no way she could have made it all the way to shore from that deep, without any air left in those little lungs. Got it? Also, don't you remember how much damn chum we threw into the water with her? That would have at least called upon a dozen flesh hungry sharks."

His words seemed to have calmed her down to some extent. "Are you sure about that?"

"Absolutely. Now, are we done?"

She let out a heavy sigh. "Yes. I probably only imagined whoever that woman was, to be Vanessa. I panicked. I'm sorry, John."

"Did you deliver the package?"

She regained her self-control and responded with a formal, professional tone in her voice. "The package is with the courier." She was usually in charge of the transactions in Durban, but this time he requested her to help him out in Cape Town. She was disappointed that this delivery took so long though. She wanted to be done and gone hours before Dwayne returned from his expedition. But there was a delay; and Dwayne had also arrived earlier than he told her he would. She hated it when she was forced to come up with a lie on the spot. She preferred well thought out, planned lies; they were much more reliable. Unfortunately, there was no time to think of a better excuse than to tell him she only came to surprise him after his long trip but her schedule only allowed her to stay a few minutes. A tiny smile appeared around her mouth as she told herself that she had probably deceived Dwayne equally successfully as in the past, since there was no reason for him not to believe her.

3

A light breeze carried the fresh aroma of the ocean through the Western Cape coastal town, Hermanus. Dwayne opened the sliding door leading to the balcony to properly see and hear the waves and smell the fresh morning air. This was something he did often and found great comfort in. Whenever he was at home between filming expeditions, he allowed himself a few minutes to sit on the balcony and get lost in the depths of the ocean, looking at the dolphins and whales playing while he enjoyed his first morning coffee.

The ringtone on his cell phone sounded louder than normal when it abruptly interrupted the silence. He glimpsed at the screen, then answered. "Terry! Please, tell me you have good news."

"Good news is all I bring." Terry sounded quite pleased with himself. "I have managed to find the address of your Vanessa. Luckily, you told me how old you think she is, because there was quite a few Vanessa Vincents who look a lot like the photo you sent me ... and between you and me, you weren't too far off with her age. She turned twenty-seven last week. I am convinced that your Vanessa and the one

I've found, is one and the same person, because this Vanessa was reported missing a week before you found your Vanessa floating in the shallows."

He wanted to tell Terry that she was not *his* Vanessa, but decided against it as he had to grab a pen and paper quickly to write down the address and contact number Terry was already providing. "What is the name of that contact person?"

"It only says mister Vincent. I have no idea if it's her spouse or her father or brother, a cousin ... it can be anyone."

"Okay, thanks."

"I hope it will shed some light."

"I'm sure it will, thank you, Terry."

His body started shivering, but not from the cool breeze. He could only hope that the address Terry gave him, was the correct one, although he believed it would be. Apparently, Terry was never wrong.

A frown appeared on his forehead as the thought crossed his mind that it was quite a coincidence that she lived in Durban, like Bernice. Why then would they have lost contact, what happened between them? All of a sudden, he was confronted by a very unwelcome and unsettling inkling. He shook his shoulders to get rid of the disturbing feeling, grabbed his keys, hurried out and jumped into his blue Toyota Land Cruiser. Well, he had to be in Durban anyway, he and May could just as well leave a day early.

On his way to Pedro's house, he convinced himself that there could be numerous reasons why

Bernice and Vanessa had lost contact. Purely because he was suspicious about Bernice's behavior, did not necessarily imply she lied to him at all.

At Pedro's, he only greeted quickly, then requested to speak to May in private.

They went outside.

"Do you truly believe I had something to do with the attempt on your life?" He looked straight into her eyes and immediately noticed the nervousness and uneasiness reflecting in them, then he asked swiftly, "Are you afraid of me?"

"I d-don't know what to think anymore." This was too emotional and upsetting to think about. She wanted to cry again, but did not know why.

He felt completely disordered. How could he take Bernice's side if all he wanted to do was protect May? Surely the possibility must exist that someone had actually tried to kill her, because, according to Terry, she was reported missing a week before he even found her.

All he cared about right now; was to clear any doubts she might have about him. "Listen, I know you are going through a tough time right now, but I really, really need you to believe me when I say that I had absolutely no involvement in that attack on your life. Think about it for a moment. Why would I try and kill you, only to save you later? If I wanted you dead, I could have easily steered Lizelle into another direction as soon as I saw you floating in the shallows, but I didn't. I immediately ran in to save you, and took you to the hospital. Why would I do that if I wanted you gone?"

"I don't know," she said in a soft, trembling voice.

He opened his mouth to continued proving his innocence, but was interrupted by his own thoughts as the question jumped into his mind: How could anyone take the life of another, in cold blood, heartless, like those people tried to take hers? A feeling of disgust flowed through him.

"Please believe me when I say you can trust me, May."

She nodded, because all of her words had run dry all of a sudden.

He took a deep breath and exhaled slowly. "I have contacted Terry, he's a private investigator, and asked his assistance. We discovered your name is Vanessa Vincent and you live in Durban." He'd rather not tell her it was Bernice who revealed her name; it would only upset her even more.

Her eyes widened as she gasped.

"Yes, and since I have to be in Durban the day after tomorrow anyway, I don't mind taking you home."

"Okay, thank you, Dwayne." Her heart started rumbling in her chest.

"Let's quickly inform your family that you are safe and that I will bring you home. Terry managed to get a contact number too." His hand slipped into his pocket and pulled out his cell phone.

"My family? Who are they?"

"Unfortunately, I don't have any names, only a number."

"Please, don't call them."

"Why not? They'll be extremely worried about you by now. Knowing you are found and on your way back home, will put an end to their nightmare."

"I know, but ... please, don't!" Terror reflected on her face, her eyes were open wide and her skin turned pale.

"Okay, okay. Relax, May." Slowly he returned his cell phone to his pocket. "We won't call them. We'll surprise them with your arrival."

They returned to Dwayne's house shortly after breakfast, where he threw a few pieces of clothes into a bag and put it next to his laptop. Then he made a few phone calls.

As the day progressed, May systematically began to accept his word that he had nothing to do with the attack on her life; and her nerves calmed down to some extent.

At six that evening Dwayne was finally ready to leave and they departed for Durban.

It was completely silent in his Land Cruiser.

Her mind was occupied with clutter. Dwayne had told her earlier that her actual name was Vanessa Vincent, but it did not even sound slightly familiar. Why could she remember Bernice's name, but not her own? Why was the assault the only thing she remembered?

Her mind soared into another direction, as mixed emotions about the current situation rumbled through her core. She was excited to finally go home, but what if she didn't recognize any of her family members? What if it brought back no memory? She was almost convinced that that was going to be the case, because the address did not ring a bell either.

Dwayne was also trapped in *his* thoughts. He found it impossible to believe that Bernice was capable of such unspeakable things. He was convinced that the 'memory' May experienced on the yacht, was only a fabrication of her mind – because she remembered Bernice in that moment, but wrongly connected her to the attempt on her life. Nevertheless, he had come to the conclusion earlier today that whether it was true or not, for May it was a frightening reality at this point in time.

"Let's find a place to sleep for a while, I'm getting tired. We'll continue our journey in the morning." He preferred driving to flying, because he believed that driving was a great way to fully connect with your inner self. It also created the time to engage with emotions and thoughts you did not want to confront otherwise. If possible, he never travelled the same route twice, even to destinations he often visited ... and whenever he could, he avoided the national highway too. This allowed him to have a clear mind when he arrived somewhere, and besides, he explored more of the country this way. Nevertheless, he stuck to the national highway for this trip.

She nodded her head, then glimpsed at the clock on the radio and noticed to her surprise it was half-past-one already.

* * * * * * * * * *

At dawn they hit the road again. The sun was just raising its head over the horizon. Dwayne seemed exhausted; he obviously did not get nearly enough rest during the past few hours.

They travelled in silence again.

She stared into the distance only seeing her thoughts; her seat slightly reclined.

After quite some time, she gasped audibly and her body moved forward as she straightened her back instantaneously.

"Adelaide," she said barely louder than her breath. She gazed out of the window, not realizing that she had spoken aloud.

"What's that?" He was lost in his own thoughts too; he hardly heard her mumbling.

She looked at him, frowning, astounded that he actually reacted to the word that was only roaming in her head. "Adelaide Harrison. My name is Adelaide Harrison!" she said delighted and extremely excited that she had finally remembered her name. Relief flashed through her veins like the first sip of hot coffee on a snowy day. "That's why the name Vanessa

Vincent didn't sound familiar, I am not her. I am Adelaide Harrison."

He jerked his head towards her, flabbergasted. His heart missed three beats, then sank as far down as his feet. He could feel every heavy beat of his heart against his ribcage.

"No. You are Vanessa Vincent." Since Terry confirmed this, he did not even once consider the possibility that she wasn't.

"No, I am not."

A feeling of distress tangled with the sensation of disappointment. "You are," he whispered, more so to convince himself.

Later, when they stopped at a gas station to refuel; and May disappeared into the shop to order two takeaway coffees, Dwayne called Terry, highly upset.

"You'd better find out who is Adelaide Harrison, fast! We are going to arrive at Vanessa Vincent's house in less than four hours."

He ended the call at the exact moment May arrived back at the vehicle.

They continued their journey without him telling her about Terry's involvement in the matter. About forty-five minutes before their expected arrival time, his cell phone rang. He pulled over immediately in order to give all his attention to the call. He deliberately did not connect his phone to the handsfree system when they left the gas station, because he did not want her to listen in on this particular conversation.

Terry skipped the formalities. "There is no Adelaide Harrison. She does not exist on any records I have access to. I've even checked my international ones."

He nodded his head at the confirmation of his suspicions. "Thank you," he ended the call with his lips pursed. He feared as much. She was most likely so afraid of the unknown that her mind was starting to fill the blanks with fabrications rather than memories.

He slowly turned towards her, and spoke as sympathetically as possible. "I've asked Terry earlier to see what he can find on Adelaide Harrison, so we don't take you to the wrong address by accident."

"Then you believe me?" Her jaw dropped from pure surprise.

He held his breath for half a second, then released it slowly through his lips. "He could not find that name anywhere. Adelaide Harrison does not exist. Your name is Vanessa, and unless you want to make things even more difficult on yourself than it already is, you should really accept that."

Her eyes teared up in frustration. "That is not true! I'm telling you; I am Adelaide!"

He rolled his eyes, "Then can Adelaide please tell me where she lives?"

"No."

It took him a few moments to get his emotions under control again. "How about this - we go to the address Terry gave us, since we are almost there anyway. We'll have a look around and see if you perhaps know anything, and whether the people living there recognize you. If not, we'll take it from there. Does that sound acceptable?"

She nodded hesitantly. "Sure." To be honest, she did not even want to go to that house. All she wanted was for him to take her back to his, or even Petro's, but she knew he wouldn't, even if she asked him to.

4

They finally arrived at the address which was apparently her home.

She opened the door of the Land Cruiser and got out tremendously slowly. She studied the grey painted house. It was not small, nor large. Then she turned her attention to the neat, medium sized yard. There was one huge tree more or less in the middle of the lawn, and flower beds all along the white palisade fence. Not extravagant at all, but beautiful in its simplicity. Nothing seemed familiar though.

They approached the gate together, and he rang the bell.

He glanced at her briefly and noticed an expression of fear on her face. She seemed exhausted and his heart contracted.

A woman peered out the front door. Almost immediately she opened the remote-controlled gate and called out, "Madam Vanessa!" While she ran towards them, she cried out with great joy, "Milady has returned!" She embraced May with tears in her eyes. "We thought we would never see you again. Come, I'll go and make you coffee."

May uncomfortably wiggled herself loose from the woman's embrace and gave a step backwards. "Who are you?"

She snapped her tongue. "But Madam, it's me, Joanna, I've been working for you for more than a year already."

Dwayne saw the confusion on May's face, and reacted swiftly. "She has total memory loss, Joanna. She cannot remember anything or anybody."

Joanna stood in reflection for a few seconds, then said, apparently to herself, "I must phone immediately." She twirled around without further ado and disappeared into the house.

May gaped at Dwayne, clearly upset at him for telling Joanna she couldn't remember anything at all, because she had already told him she remembered her name.

"Come," he insisted, seemingly not troubled by the daggers her eyes threw at him.

It appeared Joanna was home alone, because no one else came to meet them outside or when they entered. Photographs of her and a particular man greeted them when they set foot in the foyer. There were photos everywhere. Some of them also included other strangers. She walked slowly from photo frame to photo frame, frowning. She did not know any of those people. Neither the photos nor the house opened any locked away memories.

Dwayne, meanwhile, had come to a halt in front of a large portrait hanging on the wall in the lounge. A wedding photo of her and the same man in all the other pictures. Movement at the door caught his eye.

It was May entering.

She walked all the way to his side, then noticed the wedding photo and reacted sharply, "I don't know this man. This is not my husband. I am not married to anyone! Where did he get all these pictures of me?"

He could not quite comprehend why she could remember Bernice in one single glance, but failed to recognize or remember her own husband.

"May," he whispered, his mind running around like a child in desperate need of Ritalin.

A man burst through the door and called out, obviously relieved, "Vanessa!" He approached her with wide open arms, but she took a step backwards and avoided his touch. He came to a halt, then lowered his arms to his sides. "What's wrong, Vanessa?"

Dwayne recognized him as the man in the wedding photo, and spoke quickly, "Hey, I'm Dwayne Foster."

He glared at Dwayne. "Marco Vincent."

"Pleased to meet you, Marco."

Marco hesitated for a moment, trying to figure out what was going on. He was ecstatic when Joanna called with the news that Vanessa had returned. She had been missing for more than six weeks already. And now she was back, with another man, not even a bit glad to see him; not even greeting or embracing him. She only stood there like a statue, staring at him with a dazed look on her face.

He turned his attention back to the man who was standing next to her.

Dwayne explained, before he could even ask the question, "She almost drowned in the ocean about five weeks ago. I came across her body in the early hours of the morning, she was unconscious at the time. I took her to Mossel Bay hospital where she stayed for four weeks. When she regained consciousness a few days after she was admitted, it became apparent that she has total loss of memory. She cannot remember anything – not her name, her family, her address, nothing."

She spoke hastily with a bewildered look in her eyes. "I've already told you my name is Adelaide and I am not married to anyone!"

"Your name is Vanessa and you are married." A frown appeared on Marco's forehead as he wondered how she got to be in Mossel Bay. Shivers ran down his spine.

"Why is no one believing me?" She was now almost hysterical.

"Because you are Vanessa and you are married to me," he said, equally unsettled. He turned his eyes towards Dwayne, "I reported her missing a month and a half ago already. How is it possible that you have no knowledge of this? Did you not see any of the thousands of pictures we have distributed, or heard any of the reports?"

"I have been at her bedside the entire time. As a matter of fact, Marco, we notified the press immediately upon finding her to help us track down her family. But there was only a small article on her in the local paper." He remembered how upset he was when the dead dolphin, spat out by the ocean onto the beach, created a bigger commotion than the woman who had nearly drowned close by. The dead dolphin made the national television news that evening, but not a word was said about the unconscious young woman who was found, and that her family was being looked for. In fact, he was still disappointed and upset in the press, since they did not give a damn about the important things.

Marco glanced at Vanessa, and then shifted his eyes back to Dwayne. He did not trust him or the situation at all. "So, tell me, if she has no memory whatsoever, how did you find this place?" He headed for the couch presumably meant for the 'head of the house' and sat down.

Dwayne too sat down on the dark grey leather couch, after he had removed the bright blue scatter cushion. "The day before yesterday, when we returned from a week at sea, my fiancée saw her for the first time and recognized her as an old school friend. She told me her name and I contacted a private investigator to trace her address."

She tensed up and almost let out a scream of shock at this revelation, but she forced herself to keep it in and see how Marco reacted to the news.

A million questions burst through Marco's mind all at once. Why were they on the ocean for a week, instead of actively trying to figure out who she was? Who was his fiancée and why did she claim she knew Vanessa from school? That was impossible ... unless, of course, his fiancée was Bernice, which in return implied Dwayne was the man who ...

He got a massive shock by this disclosure. His heartbeat started racing. How dared this scumbag came into his house! Why did he decide to bring her back now, all of a sudden? Did she talk?

"Oh really?" He lifted his eyebrows high into his forehead, and the tone in his voice signaled that he did not believe Dwayne. "So, who is this fiancée of yours and when *exactly* was she friends with Vanessa?"

Dwayne ignored his attitude and answered calmly, "Bernice O'Brian. She told me that she and Vanessa were friends many years ago, but they'd lost contact about five years ago."

The confirmation hit him like a blow in the stomach, but he was an expert in maintaining self-control. "Now that is very interesting."

"What is so interesting about it?"

"What were you doing on the ocean for a week?" He glimpsed at Vanessa. She had taken a seat on the opposite side of the lounge and was as silent and as pale as death itself (well, what he imagined the grim reaper would look like under those robes). He felt sorry for her and longed to take her in his arms, even if only for a brief moment. However, he had no idea what was going on, and the fact that he could not read her body language, made matters worse. In the past, she would only give him one look or pulled her mouth in a certain way, and he would know immediately what she was trying to tell him ... but now, he could not read her at all and that made him feel vulnerable.

When Dwayne started answering his question, he tore his eyes away from her and looked back at him. "We were filming the new season for *Know your coastline– along the deep sea*. I am co-host of this show and we used your wife as inspiration for a new approach to the new season. She will even have an appearance, but as May Neeman of course, as we used to call her then because her name was unknown."

"Under no circumstances will that happen!" He was so derailed by this, that he completely forgot everything he was thinking about and that he was testing Dwayne to figure out his involvement.

"Oh really, and why not?" Dwayne snaped back, fed-up with this man's rudeness.

"It's out of the question; you have no consent to use her name or face in your show."

"On the contrary, Marco, she has given us the necessary consent and you do not have the authority to overrule it, even as her spouse."

"When she gave her consent, she was not in the right mental state to do so! I forbid you to use any footage of her! Your team will have to edit her out. You can use old footage, or reshoot the whole thing, but Vanessa is not to be a part of it."

"I can't. We have already lost too much time with my supporting her in hospital. And it has been edited already."

"I don't care! That footage will not appear on television. You have no idea what the consequences will be if you disobey me!"

"*This* is the thanks I get?" Dwayne raised his voice to match that of Marco.

Not even a second passed after he had spoken those words before Marco was on his feet. He gestured that Dwayne did the same. He was seemingly no longer welcome in his house.

Dwayne glanced at Vanessa who had not yet uttered a word. She seemed so frightened and helpless, he had to force himself not to ask her to leave with him, back to Hermanus. He hated the idea of leaving her alone with this unpleasant, rude human being, who obviously ruled her life with an iron fist.

Marco headed towards the front door, gesturing to Dwayne to follow.

Finally, Vanessa spoke, looking straight at Marco. "Dwayne has been driving through the entire night to get me home safely. The least you can do, is have him stay the night."

Dwayne shook his head. "I'll be fine, thank you, May..."

"And I'll be grateful towards him for bringing you back home safely forever, Vanessa," Marco interrupted, ignoring Dwayne completely. "But ..."

"He has done so much more than *that*," she interrupted him in return, although her eyes had moved to meet those of Dwayne, as if she was addressing him. An almost invisible smile touched her lips.

Marco tensed up, instantly suspicious again. What did she mean by *that*?

She continued speaking, all the time keeping eye contact with Dwayne. "Not only did he save my life, but he spent every moment he possibly could, at my bedside, which he was under no obligation to do. He gave me a place to stay when I did not have any. Plus, the moment he found out my actual name, he did everything in his power to locate my family and address. Then he altered his schedule to bring me home first."

She paused. "He most certainly did not *just* bring me home safely."

Dwayne smiled at her, then opened his mouth to speak, but Marco's toneless voice silenced him. "Thank you for the effort, Dwayne."

Marco was annoyed. Why did she have to make such a big deal of this guy? The sudden eruption of jealousy sent a burning sensation through his chest. It caught him by surprise though, since he'd never been jealous of her before. The pain in his chest became more intense. He blamed that feeling on the guilt and remorse he felt over the past month and a half. If only he had listened to her the day before she disappeared, things would have been so different. If only he had heeded her words and not took them as naïve, over-reactive and misreading of the situation, this would never have happened. It was only when she did not return home that he realized how wrong he was.

He pulled himself back from the past, and it took everything within him to keep his composure. "I truly mean it when I say I'm grateful, Dwayne, even though you might think differently. Also, asking you to cut her out of your show, is to protect you – not her, not me, but *you*. You have no idea what you are going to get yourself involved in, if you go ahead and keep her in your show. Believe me; you don't want to go there. In fact, Dwayne, I'd advise you to forget this ever happened. Forget you met Vanessa, forget that she even exists. It will be much better for you this way. Turn around, leave this place and live the rest of your life in peace."

Dwayne was on the verge of punching this bad-mannered bloke in the face. But he only shook his head instead. "Goodbye, May, I mean, Vanessa." Then he exited the house. He could not explain why he felt so empty all of a sudden.

The moment he unlocked his vehicle, Marco spoke from behind him, "Wait! Vanessa will never forgive me if I let you go now. You can stay to catch up on lost sleep. But tomorrow, you're gone." He would much rather have shouted: 'good-riddance!', but he didn't want to upset Vanessa even more.

Dwayne opened his mouth, ready to reject the forced invitation, when he caught a glimpse of Vanessa's face, and decided against it. "Okay, thank you."

They went back inside, but for the rest of Dwayne's stay, Marco did everything in his power to prevent him spending even a second in Vanessa's company unsupervised – like the helicopter parent on a teenager's first date.

The night was still young when Vanessa turned towards Marco. "I did not really get much sleep last night either. I'm going to bed now. I'll use one of the guest rooms."

He frowned, clearly not pleased. "Why the guest room?"

"Are you really asking me this, Marco? Can't you figure it out for yourself?"

"I'm sorry, I wasn't thinking straight. Of course you can use one of the guest rooms. Let me show you."

He took her to the room closest to the main bedroom where he could keep an eye on her throughout the night.

Then he returned to the lounge and took his seat. "Tell me again, how and when exactly did you find Vanessa?"

"About five weeks ago, I was visiting my sister in Mossel Bay. We went for a jog that morning, earlier than usual. That was when I saw her floating body in the shallow waters on the beach. As I told you already, she was unconscious and when she regained her consciousness, she was suffering from amnesia."

"It's hard to believe, you know?"

"I understand completely, Marco. At first, I found it hard to believe myself. But she truly can't remember anything."

"So, what do you think, how did she end up in the water?"

"I initially thought she was a tourist who went swimming and got swept away by a current. But she doesn't remember going for a swim that morning." Since he did not know for a fact that there actually was an attack on her life, he rather kept that information to himself.

"So how is it possible that your fiancée only met her two days ago while you rescued her five weeks ago already?"

"Because we haven't seen each other for quite some time. She is a teacher here in Durban and I live in Hermanus. To be honest, we barely see each other. She was here in Durban, working, when I found Vanessa. Also, Bernice never accompanies me when I am busy filming. When we returned from our last expedition, Bernice was waiting for me at the harbor in Cape Town to pay me a surprise visit, and it was *then* when she saw Vanessa and recognized her."

He nodded his head. "If you say you barely see each other, what exactly does it mean?"

"It means we only see each other once or twice for a few hours every couple of months. The school keeps her quite busy."

"Am I to understand from this, that you don't accompany her to any of her functions?"

"You understand correctly, yes. Why do you ask?"

"I am only curious. You mentioned you are co-host of the TV-show, who is your partner?"

"Pedro Oliver. Have you not seen our show?"

"No. Where does Pedro live?"

"In De Kelders."

"I see, so, with you living in Hermanus and Pedro in De Kelders, where does your team finalize the production of your show?"

"We have a studio in my backyard. Pedro is currently busy with the final touches while I'm here in Durban to attend a meeting. One of us had to stay and do it, because we have to submit our final product in a couple of days for the show to be broadcasted per schedule. Will you excuse me? I want to go and sleep now."

"Of course. Let me show you to your room."

Marco pulled Dwayne's room's door shut behind him, convinced that he had no part in Vanessa's disappearance. As a result of his profession, he had closed his heart to the feelings and problems of others, but surprisingly, he felt sorry for Dwayne.

"Poor guy, he has no idea what's coming," he whispered to himself as he entered the main bedroom.

5

The moment Dwayne's Land Cruiser vanished around the corner the next morning, Marco and Vanessa headed back to the house. His brown eyes filled with concern. The tension he had been through the past month and a half, made him appear considerably older than his thirty-one years of age.

A miserable feeling took hold of him. He knew all too well what was going to happen if she did not regain her memory fast. In the past, that specific clause never bothered him, but now things had taken a turn for the worse, affecting him directly. If only he knew how to help her recover her memory without telling her everything, because that would be fatal.

If he enlightened her, and someone found out later that he had told her, his fate would be the same as hers. She had to remember everything of her own accord, or else it would be both their heads on the chopping block.

"Can I ask you something, Vanessa?" He approached this with great care as they reached the front door.

"Yes."

"Do you honestly remember nothing at all? If there is something, I need you to tell me now. Also, when you remember anything new, no matter when, no matter what, no matter how small, it's really important that you tell me immediately." He was genuinely worried. He had noticed how pale she was ever since she arrived yesterday. Hopefully she only pretended in Dwayne's company that she couldn't remember anything, for whatever reason...

She turned her head and stared into the distance, trying her best to convince herself that she had made a mistake earlier ... that she actually *was* Vanessa and married to Marco, because, yesterday, he seemed truly relieved and genuinely happy to see her. Surely, he would not have reacted that way if she wasn't.

He also provided evidence that he was telling the truth; he had shown her ID document as well as their marriage certificate to her and Dwayne. She had noticed how he watched her, staring at her facial features, clearly longing for her.

She broke loose from her thoughts. "To be honest, there actually is something I remembered, but that's probably only my imagination too."

"Why would you think that?"

"Because I was convinced that I am Adelaide Harrison and that I'm unmarried ... and I was completely wrong, why would this 'memory' be any different?"

He placed his hand on her shoulder, but she shook it off. This hurt and upset him greatly. "Maybe it is, maybe it isn't, but I have to know anyway. Besides, you are my wife, and if I think that what you say is not true, I'll tell you. Please, tell me what it is you remember."

She hesitated for a moment. "During the time we were on Dwayne's yacht, I was still totally without memory. Initially, I was afraid to get onto the yacht, because it felt as if it posed a threat to me. I assumed I was only scared because I had almost drowned in the ocean. However, when we returned to the harbor, I saw Bernice and I immediately recognized her. I instantly remembered how she and two other men were assaulting me on a yacht. I remember them shouting insults at me while they forced me into swimwear, all the time hurting me. They then tied weights onto me. One of the two men tried to drug me with something, but Bernice stopped him. *'Don't have mercy on her. Make her suffer,'* she said. Then they threw me overboard. I remember how I struggled to escape from the weights and how I tried to surface but it was practically impossible. I vaguely remember a dolphin coming to my rescue, but I lost consciousness and am not entirely sure how I ended up on shore. Maybe I was only hallucinating the part of the dolphin, or maybe the entire ordeal. I just don't know."

She stopped talking for a moment and wiped the tears from her cheeks. "Do you think there is a possibility that this actually happened?"

His heart was filled with regret, guilt and self-loathing. It was all his fault. He should not have let her go with Bernice alone. He had so much more experience than her and he should have known that things might not go smoothly.

"I believe every word you say, Vanessa, and yes, I think something like that could have happened."

"Why?"

"Because ... people do get kidnapped and assaulted, it is not unheard of, and sometimes they end up somewhere strange. I am truly sorry that something like this has happened to you." He paused. "Who were the two men with Bernice?" If she could supply their names, it would be the breakthrough he had been looking for, for a long time.

"I don't know. I can't even remember their faces. They are all blurry, except for Bernice."

He pursed his lips, disappointed, then tried to comfort her. "It's okay, it doesn't matter. You'll remember them soon enough. Promise me you will tell me immediately when you remember who they were, please, Vanessa? It is extremely important."

"I promise I will tell you immediately, Marco."

* * * * * * * * * *

While Dwayne and Marcell discussed important matters, Dwayne's mind slipped away. He was relieved that it turned out May was indeed Vanessa, and that the address Terry had given him was correct. He trusted that her memory would return quickly now that she was back in a familiar place. ... Bernice's face popped-up in his mind as if she was there in person. What would her reaction be if she knew he had spent the night at Vanessa's house? No, he decided promptly, he would not tell her he came to Durban earlier than planned, it might only complicate things.

He brought his attention back to the current conversation when Marcell asked in a loud voice, "Are you fine with this arrangement?"

"Of course, that is perfect. Would you mind emailing the information to Pedro as well?" Although he had no idea what he agreed to, he was confident it would be in order. He was definitely not going to admit to Marcell that he did not hear a single word he had said or that *he* only responded unconsciously during their discussion. Obviously, Marcell was happy with the result, which indicated he did not notice that Dwayne's attention was somewhere else.

"I'll send it to Pedro, yes. Thank you, Dwayne."

He got up from his chair and shook Marcell's hand. "Thank you. We'll be in touch."

When he arrived at Bernice's house, she did not seem thrilled to see him at all. Even her voice conveyed the message that his timing was terrible. "I should have told you that I am very busy and that I won't have time for you today."

"I won't take up too much of your time. I only wanted to see you quickly, I miss you." If he had to be honest with himself, he had actually been thinking more about Vanessa these past few days than *her*. A guilty feeling sneaked up his chest because he did not miss Bernice as much as he made it sound.

She shrugged as though she couldn't care less; she didn't even say she missed him too.

He pursed his lips briefly. "It's such lovely weather today, maybe I'll go for a swim before I head back home."

Silence followed. She stared into the distance, seemingly lost in thought.

"You know, it's not fair that your principal demands so much of your free time. What are the other teachers doing? Are they also this busy?"

She chewed on a nail, obviously nervous about something, virtually unaware of his presence.

He narrowed his eyes, observing her behavior intensely. Then he scrutinized the living room with his eyes and noticed that on the coffee table were two cell phones.

"Is there someone else here?" He could not help but wonder if *that* was the reason she apparently was so busy today – did he perhaps interrupt her and another man?

"No one else is here. I have to be at school for sport in fifteen minutes, excuse me while I go get dressed in my sportwear."

He waited for her to disappear into her room, then jumped at the opportunity and grabbed the unknown cell phone from the table. For a brief moment he gazed at the device in his hands, not quite sure how he would be able to unlock it. Then, in the heat of the moment, he entered her standard pin number. To his surprise, it worked, and he quickly browsed through the contact list. He did not recognize any of the names. He was about to access her messages when the door of her room opened. He swiftly put it back where he found it and went back to his seat, pretending he had never even seen it.

Before she had even entered the living room properly, she started to speak, "I think it would be best if you leave now. I will be gone for hours, and be too tired to entertain you when I return."

"Very well, Bernice. Then I'll see you when I see you." He walked out, got into his Land Cruiser and left, battling to organize his chaotic thoughts.

* * * * * * * * *

A couple of police officials burst into the studio where Pedro was busy working and waved their identification cards in his face.

"We are here to confiscate the footage of your latest trip," said the man who had introduced himself as Captain Brett.

"Excuse me, Captain, but we did not do or record anything illegal. What is your reason for this?"

The only response he received, was the officials scavenging through everything without caring about the mess or damage they caused. When they could not find what they were looking for, Captain Brett turned towards Pedro and barked, "If you don't cooperate, I will arrest you right here and now!"

"Why? I have done nothing criminal. In fact, I am still waiting for you to tell me why you want the footage?"

"That is confidential information! This is a high-profile case, and if you do not hand over the footage, you will be arrested immediately! You don't want to spend the rest of your life in prison for something you can easily go out and film again, do you?"

"No, Captain." With shaking hands, he handed over their hard work unwillingly.

"There we go," said Captain Brett with a tiny smile around his lips. "Are there any other copies, or back-ups of this?" He raised his eyebrows and pushed his chest out, intimidatingly.

"That is all we have."

"Now you listen to me, boy, if you lied and you go ahead and broadcast any footage containing Vanessa Vincent, or even mention her name, there will be severe consequences. Not only will you lose all rights to air anything ever again, you'll also be arrested. You got that?"

Pedro nodded, too stunned to respond.

Just as rapidly as they appeared, they were gone.

He was frozen for a substantial amount of time, paralyzed with shock, before he could move again. He grabbed his cell phone from his pocket. The moment the call went through, he yelled anxiously, "DWAYNE!"

"What? What? Calm down." Then he started to panic – something horrible must have happened to send his friend over the edge like that. He quickly pulled over to the side of the road and stopped his vehicle.

"They took everything, mate. Everything!"

"Who took what, Pedro? What are you talking about?"

"The police, man, they came and took everything we have on our latest filming."

"What?!"

"All our footage! They ambushed me!"

"They have no right to take anything without a warrant. Did they have a warrant?"

"I don't know! They wanted to arrest me. They said I'll spend my life behind bars if I don't give it to them."

"But why?"

"It's got something to do with that woman of yours; Vanessa! They said if we show any footage of her or even mention her name, we'll never be able to broadcast anything ever again, mate. How do they even know we've got her in the footage? We were supposed to keep her appearance a surprise, man! Did you tell anyone?"

Dwayne was instantly annoyed because Pedro, like Terry, called her "his", but he was not going to react on that, neither to the question whether he had told anyone. "Listen Pedro, why can't she be on television, what did they say?"

"Nothing! Apparently, it's confidential information. What are we going to do now? There is no way we'll have enough time to go out and re-film everything?"

"Just give me time to think." He ended the call abruptly, highly upset. His entire body shuddered from anger. He took a few deep breaths, forcing himself to calm down. When his anger had abated enough for him to think straight again, he started analyzing the bizarre situation.

Then it hit him, there could only be one person behind this. Marco.

"How dare he?" He cried out loud to no one. Who did he think he was? Of course he did not plan on listening to that bastard and cut Vanessa from the recordings. ... But how could he have known that he was going to broadcast it anyway?

He pursed his lips in anger. How did Marco manage to get the police to do this so quickly? Were they even real police officers?

The trip back home took forever. The hours passed ever so slowly. He made a call to Pedro, asking him to work through some old footage and see if he could find something useful in the meantime. He would help him with that as soon as he returned.

* * * * * * * * * *

Marco met Captain Brett the next day in the park as they had arranged earlier.

"Here are the recordings you wanted." Brett handed him an opaque plastic bag.

"Is this everything?"

"The whole lot," he confirmed.

"Thanks."

"Pleasure," Brett said, then disappeared casually.

* * * * * * * * * *

"I bet Marco is behind this entire business of our recordings being confiscated!" Dwayne said, infuriated, when he arrived back home and entered the studio.

"Who is Marco, mate?"

"Vanessa's husband."

Pedro scratched his head. "Why would he be behind this?"

"Because his wife was filmed and he hated the idea of her being on television."

"I don't know, mate, when I asked the police their reason for confiscating our work, they said it's a high-profile case. They said nothing about her husband or that he was behind this."

"I doubt they were actual police officers, Pedro. My guess is Marco contacted someone who probably owes him a favor to do this."

Pedro gazed at him, frowning. "You really think so?"

"Yes, I have met the guy, remember. He is the most unreasonable man I have ever encountered and the poor Vanessa undoubtedly has no say in anything. Maybe she remembered him after all, and that's the reason she didn't want to go home in the first place. I won't even blame her for not confessing to it. You should have seen her. She looked so scared. I got the impression he is a total control freak."

"That is so sad."

"Indeed. If I could, I would have brought her back with me."

Pedro's eyebrows raised. "Really?"

"Really."

"On a different note, I thought we decided to contribute five percent of our profit on this season to nature conservation in Durban, as we always do to any organization who approach us for donations."

"We did, yes."

"Then why did you and Marcell settle on ten percent?"

A frown appeared between his eyes. "Ten?"

"Yes, mate, ten."

His jaw dropped; no wonder Marcell seemed rather pleased with their arrangement. "I'm so sorry, this is all my fault. To be honest, I didn't give much attention to Marcell when we discussed this matter. I didn't realize that I agreed to ten percent rather than five."

"Luckily, it's only on this season's profit, and he committed to give professional insight whenever we plan on filming in and around Durban. But why weren't you paying attention?"

With a guilty look on his face, he replied, "I was thinking about Vanessa ..."

Pedro waited for him to continue, but when it became clear that Dwayne was not going to elaborate, he nodded his head. "I see. Vanessa ..."

They struggled for a few days to find something on their old shoots that could be used for the new season. Something that was good enough so that they could still go on air on time.

The more they worked through the old material, the more Dwayne knew that it was not even close to the standard expected of them for this season. They were running the risk that they might lose a huge percentage of their audience which they might never get back.

"If I get my hands on that man, I'll do something to him. No person in his right mind would do such a cruel thing to ruin our career purely for selfish reasons." Dwayne's annoyance with Marco flared yet again.

"Why so aggressive, mate, this is so unlike you?"

"Can you imagine what he is doing to Vanessa? I can! He's probably beating her because she agreed to be filmed and appear on our show."

A smile touched Pedro's lips. "Oh, now I get it. It's because you think Vanessa might be suffering under his hand."

"How could he treat her this bad?"

"You don't even know if it's actually true, mate. Calm down."

Dwayne shook his head; it only made him angrier when told to calm down. He took a break and went for a walk outside. When he returned, he continued looking through old footage again. As soon as he identified anything usable, he passed it on to Pedro who pieced everything together. Each episode needed to be unique in its own right, but also had to fit in with the overall theme of the season in whole.

"I think we should call it a day," said Dwayne later.

"Agree! We are almost done, and can do the final touches tomorrow."

Pedro spent the night at Dwayne's house so they could start working as early as possible the next morning. Time was of the essence as they did not want to miss the deadline.

Before breakfast they were already back in the studio.

"Do you think Vanessa would like this?" Dwayne asked a few minutes after they started working.

Pedro shifted his attention from his laptop screen to that of Dwayne's, glancing at the picture of a short-tail stingray, the largest stingray species. "Oh yes, definitely. In fact, I think she would love it." He smiled, amused, as he was essentially waiting for Dwayne to mention her name. Ever since he had returned from Durban, he had talked about her. Every single day.

"Me too. You know, she loved the footage of the sea-creatures way more than those of the non-natural treasures we found in the ocean."

"I know. Would you like to include that into the last episode as well? I am almost done with it now, but I can change it quickly if you wish."

"Yes, let's include this too, thank you, Pedro."

He made the necessary changes and then they were finally done with everything, just in time to meet the deadline.

Dwayne sighed relieved, then steered the conversation into a different direction. "You know, Pedro, when I was visiting Bernice the other day, I found an unfamiliar cell phone on her table. I secretly scrolled through the contact list, and there was not a single familiar name on it."

"So? I bet you don't know all the names on my contact list either."

"That's not the point. That particular cell phone was right next to hers on the table. So, either she had company that day, someone who has the exact same pin on their phone as her, or she has a cell phone with a bunch of people she doesn't want me to know about. Either way, she is hiding something from me."

"And from the expression on your face, I assume you didn't ask her about it?"

"No."

"Why not?"

"Because!"

"You know very well that 'because' is not an answer, mate."

"I don't know what's going on, but something is wrong. Lately, she is too busy to give any attention to me. She hardly calls me anymore. She literally chased me away the last time I was there, and I had arranged that visit in advance. Why was I not welcome on that particular day? I can't help being skeptical, Pedro. Especially after she bought an airplane ticket, flew all the way to Cape Town only to see me for a few moments, while she knew I would be visiting her three days later. And all that on a teacher's salary? I don't know, man, something about this is off."

"It does sound suspicious, but you should discuss it with her. Maybe there is a perfectly good explanation for everything."

"You think there can be a logical explanation for this?"

"There might just be, but how will you ever know if you only go on your assumptions?"

He sighed, "You are probably right. I'll call her."

6

For the first time in many years Marco took two consecutive weeks' vacation and tried everything in his power to help Vanessa regain her memory. He took her to some of her favorite restaurants; to places they'd been together before. He showed her every photo ever taken of them and told her a short story about each one, without blurting out anything that could get them into trouble. He was tempted more than once to tell her everything, but he managed to resist. However, all his attempts were fruitless.

By the time his vacation came to an end, she had not regained any other memory whatsoever.

A few days after he went back to office, he knew he could no longer protect her. The questions and pressure from his superior were becoming more intense every single day. He had no other choice left. This broke his heart. His emotions were running wildly between anger, pity and remorse, so much so it drained his energy. If only he could resign, take Vanessa and vanish with her, but it would make no difference, he knew.

He tried one last time. "Vanessa, is there truly nothing else you remember?"

"No." It felt as though someone had draped her mind with a cloak, hiding every single memory and experience she had ever had.

"There's something I need to tell you."

"Yes?"

"Before your disappearance, you used to work in the Police Force, like me."

She frowned. "Was I really?"

"Yes."

"Why haven't you told me this before?"

"Because it would have influenced your memory. I wanted you to remember of your own accord. Unfortunately it did not happen, so I am telling you now."

"But ... there is not a single police uniform in my closet. And I didn't even know you were a police officer. Why don't you wear uniform?"

"Well, none of our positions require us to wear uniform."

"What positions is that exactly?"

He hesitated for a brief moment, considering how much to tell her, but decided against it. "Will you come with me to work tomorrow, please, Vanessa?"

Her eyes rested on his face. He seemed agitated and while she did not want to go to his office, she agreed.

They left early the next morning. As they walked through the corridor, he took her hand, and for some unexplained reason, she allowed him. His sudden change of mood, as well as the strange expression in his eyes, prevented her from pulling her hand from his.

He glanced at her with his heart in his throat, he had stalled this moment for as long as possible.

Most of the people seemed glad and delighted to see her again. She did not recognize any of them. Marco did his best to introduce everyone as casually as possible. Then they continued to the next desk or office. She did not speak much, only apologized for not remembering them. She had no idea why he deemed it necessary for her to accompany him today. Why was it so important to him? Did he actually think *this* would trigger her memory?

After a while she noticed he started walking slower and stayed a little longer at each person's desk before continuing. From the looks of it, he was actually becoming tenser by the minute, almost as if he was doing something against his will.

His voice interrupted her thoughts. "This is the second last office, Vanessa."

The feeling that he was losing her, was overwhelming, and the pain in his chest became unbearable. He knew, after today, he would never see her again and there was nothing he could do to change that. This was the last few moments he had with her before she would be gone forever.

All he wanted to do, was to turn around and take her back home. But it was out of the question. They had to face this, now. This was the second last office

76

before her fate would be sealed. He knew exactly what her fate would be, that was no secret after all, nevertheless, nothing in this universe could have prepared him for what was about to happen. With a heavy heart, he knocked, turned the knob, opened the door slowly and entered.

She almost let out a scream, but pursed her lips as firmly as possible; her legs became jelly. She instantly knew she could not reveal, under any circumstances, that she recognized the man behind the desk! She squeezed Marco's hand so tightly that he glimpsed at her in surprise.

The memory replayed in her head faster than lightning: *It's early morning, still dark. This man is talking to Bernice, telling her to throw a scoop of bait with her into the ocean, "You know, to attract sharks!" He turns his face towards her, laughs from his belly with delight. "Did you finally realize that yesterday morning was the last time you have ever seen a sunrise, dear?" He pushes her with so much force, she bumps into the other man with them, who in return pushes her back and she falls onto her knees on the deck.*

Marco witnessed her face paling at a spectacular rate. This not only confused him, but made him instantly concerned at the same time. Nonetheless, he kept a straight face and spoke in a neutral tone. "Vanessa, this is Lieutenant Colonel John Hall, second in command here."

John inhaled sharply and also paled up the moment he saw them. He was clearly doing everything in his power to remain calm. "Hey, Vanessa. I'm so glad to see you. You've been gone from work for quite some time. How long was it exactly?"

Marco's heartrate increased drastically as they stood in a moment of silence. *This could not be, he surely misinterpreted...*

"It's been a little more than two months, sir."

He nodded and replied in an extremely calm voice, "I see; then it is about time you start working again."

"I wouldn't know where to begin, sir, I have lost my memory." If Marco wasn't squeezing all of the blood from her fingers, she would have rushed out of there as fast as she could.

"Don't worry, Marco will show you the ropes, won't you?"

The look on John's face sent shivers down his spine. "Of course. Come, Vanessa."

He steered her to the nearest door leading to privacy. When they were alone, he spoke, "what just happened in there?"

"It was him. He was one of the guys with Bernice on the yacht. He was the one in charge." It was immensely difficult not to shout that out loud.

"What?" He pulled her closer and wrapped his arms around her. *How is this possible?* Not in his wildest dreams did he see this coming. The smallest possibility that might have existed of her escaping her fate, was gone now, once and for all. John would definitely see to it personally that no exception to the rule would be made today, no doubt about that.

Never in his entire life had he ever experienced so many emotions in one single moment. His mind set off at top speed, trying to get to a solution fast. Then it dawned on him that the only way out, was to take matters into his own hands.

He whispered next to her ear. "I have to take you to Colonel Payne now. There is no getting around that, but listen closely, under no circumstances can you tell her that you remember Bernice or John or anything else. She is one of the best interrogators I have ever encountered, but you must convince her that you suffer from total amnesia. Please, Vanessa, it is of utmost importance that she believes you." If the colonel got the slightest idea that there was something Vanessa remembered, she might decide to let her stay, and he had to prevent that from happening at all cost. He had to get her away from here, instantly.

"If she's as good as you say, I might fail in convincing her." She stepped out of his embrace.

"Oh no, you did an excellent job in John's office. You can do this. Just believe in yourself as much as I do."

"Alright." She had no idea what was going on, but during the past weeks, she had learned to trust him.

He would not instruct her to do this if he did not have a good reason.

"Alright, let's go," he said.

A few minutes later they entered Colonel Payne's office. It was she who questioned him about Vanessa when his leave had come to an end. She had called him while he was busy with his assignment in the field, and demanded answers. He was caught off guard by her call. He did not tell anyone Vanessa had returned since he knew what would happen when they found out she suffered from amnesia. But the colonel alleged she had seen them together during his vacation. She turned on the heat when he confirmed that Vanessa was back but failed to elaborate. Yesterday, when she had called him again, she threatened that if he did not bring Vanessa to see her today, he left her with no other choice but to arrest her immediately. He knew Payne was not joking and that she would have no mercy on Vanessa once detained.

"Please sit, Vanessa." Colonel Payne gestured to the chair in front of her desk.

She turned her eyes towards Marco and opened her mouth to speak, presumably to ask him to leave the office, but he beat her to it, "If you don't mind, Colonel, I would like to stay. Vanessa has had a tough day so far and because of her memory loss, she is quite exhausted and vulnerable. My presence will set her at ease to talk to you. I promise I will not interfere."

She hesitated. "Very well, you can stay, but I don't want to hear one word from you. Is that clear?"

He nodded, then took a seat next to Vanessa, close enough for her to feel his presence. And strangely enough, it calmed her nerves, as he claimed it would.

Colonel Payne started her interrogation.

The questioning was very subtle, intended to lead Vanessa into a situation where she either contradicted herself or admitted that she did not suffer from total amnesia. However, she did not fall for the colonel's deceptively friendly and caring approach. If Marco hadn't warned her about her skills, she probably would have let something slip unintentionally. She paid close attention to every detail, but cautiously stuck to one answer, only rephrasing it from time to time: "I don't know, Colonel, I don't remember." She resisted the temptation to elaborate on some of the questions, and was very proud of herself for being able to do so.

Finally, the colonel was satisfied that Vanessa truly had no memory whatsoever and asked her to go and wait in Marco's office.

Colonel Payne waited for a few moments after Vanessa had closed the door before addressing Marco. "You know what you have to do, Vincent. Are you up to it, or should I get someone else to handle it?"

"No need to involve someone else, Colonel, I have been preparing myself for this for quite some time now."

"Alright then. I expect you back at work in no longer than three days."

"Sure thing, Boss." He got up and walked out. It took every ounce of strength he had, to keep calm and not run out of the office. If the colonel got even the slightest suspicion that he might disobey her orders, she would not hesitate to deal with it herself. It was she who included that ridiculous clause in the first place, when she started working at this branch.

* * * * * * * * * *

"Vanessa is alive!" John yelled this at Bernice when he called her as soon as he arrived home, much earlier than usual.

He slammed on the desk with his fist. Livid. When Bernice told him a few months ago of someone with much potential to be of great benefit to them and their business, he was very excited. But, when she told him it was Vanessa Vincent, he immediately realized that *that* was Vanessa and Marco's undercover operation and that they had orders to take them down. He then decided that he would lure her in, and let her come to her tragic end before she could do any harm. So, he arranged a meeting – one that was supposed to be her last, took her out on his yacht and threw her into the ocean.

He banged on the desk again, outraged. How the hell did she survive?

Bernice felt her legs go numb. "I told you I saw her! I told you, John, but you wouldn't listen. You did not believe me!"

"This is all your fault!"

"How dare you blame me?! How is this my fault?" Under normal circumstances she would never ever raise her voice to him, but she was angry. Furious. Desperate to defend herself.

John was beside himself with rage. If his involvement leaked, he would not only lose his job, but most definitely be imprisoned for the rest of his life.

"Of course this is your fault! You are the one that said she must not be sedated before we throw her overboard, remember? Oh, no! You wanted her to feel everything while she dies slowly. Now look where that got us!"

She tried to interrupt him, but he was storming on and on and did not even give her a moment to speak. There was absolutely no end to his monologue.

"The only reason your corpse has not joined the coral reef, is because Vanessa has lost her memory! This means that her life will come to an end today anyway. You are very lucky, brat, that she will take the memory of our involvement in this to the grave. A small upside to this, is that her blood will not be on our hands anymore." He ended the call without giving her time to respond at all.

She was left speechless, her mouth tremendously dry. Vanessa was really alive, just as she feared. Then it dawned on her that Dwayne had lied to her. *That* woman was not Pedro's girlfriend and they had definitely not been together for two months. A frown appeared between her eyes as she wondered why he would lie to her. She shook her head, then another possibility entered her mind. Maybe Pedro had told him that story, and he believed it.

Although she wanted to act promptly to determine whether Dwayne had made himself her enemy, she resisted the urge to contact him. She took a step back, mentally, and started planning. That was how she always dealt with problems. She never rushed into any situation, especially difficult ones. Her thoughts were running wildly from one possibility to another, but she could not understand how they came across Vanessa and why she was on Dwayne's yacht.

She took a deep breath, exhaled slowly and closed her eyes while convincing herself that it did not matter anymore. Because of Vanessa's amnesia, she could not have told them anything anyway, regardless of how she got there. Besides, Dwayne would be highly suspicious if she started interrogating him now.

A sudden sensation of powerlessness overcame her. She hated that feeling.

* * * * * * * * *

Dwayne gazed at the phone in his hand. It had been ages since Bernice last took any of his calls. He constantly tried to reach her, with no success. Should he even try again? He sighed, then made the call anyway.

She sounded annoyed when she answered, "Yes, Dwayne?" Since her conversation with John yesterday, the fact that he blamed her for Vanessa still being alive, together with the possibility that Dwayne might have lied to her, had put her in a real bad mood.

Her rudeness infuriated him, but he tried his best to remain friendly. "Hello, Bernice..."

"What do you want?"

He clenched his jaw before answering, "I wanted to hear how you are doing. You've been so quiet lately. I haven't heard from you for weeks now."

"I'm fine. Is there something important you wanted to discuss? I'm really busy and don't have time for children's games."

It had never been her idea to ask him to marry her. She didn't even believe in love. It was John who instructed her to propose. He had high hopes that they could include Dwayne in their business since he knew the ocean so well and had his own yacht which would have made deliveries so much easier. However, it became very clear, very quickly, that Dwayne would not be interested in their operation. So, she never even made the suggestion to him. Since she discovered that he would not join them, she had no use for him anymore. That was why she started to tell him that her work took up all of her time. She had actually hoped he would get tired of trying, and end the engagement, but instead, he became quite annoyingly needy. She did not want to end it herself after being the one who proposed, because she did not want to raise suspicion or create any unnecessary attention and questions that could expose her. Why could he not get the message and end this useless relationship?

"No, Bernice, there is nothing important I wanted to discuss. I only wanted to say 'Hello,' you know." He ended the call right there and then, relatively mad. First, she ignored him for weeks, and then, when she finally took his call, this was how she treated him.

Pedro looked up from his work, surprised. "What now? Why are you being so rude to her?"

"Rude, me? You should have heard the way she talked to me, man. I am tired of her disrespectful behavior."

Pedro widened his eyes and lifted his eyebrows as far as they could go.

A few moments of silence passed before Dwayne spoke again. "Do you think Vanessa has regained her memory yet?"

"What made you think of her now?" It was not strange anymore that Dwayne thought or talked about Vanessa all the time, but he did find it odd that Dwayne's thoughts would meander to her during a seemingly unpleasant conversation with Bernice.

"Nothing specifically. You know, even when she accused me of attempted murder, she did not treat me as bad as Bernice does."

"Oh, now I understand."

"Excuse me?"

"Why don't you call Vanessa and ask her if she has recovered her memory, mate?"

"I don't have her number, and even if I did ..."

"You must remind me to introduce you to my friend, Terry. He has quite the talent for finding out any information he wants."

"Don't be silly! I am not going to ask a private investigator to get me a married woman's number. Besides, you have seen how unreasonable her husband is." Of course he had the cell phone number Terry provided back then, but there was no way he would make a call to that number; besides, Marco would definitely not let him speak to her even if he did.

Pedro laughed, then gave Dwayne a pat on the shoulder as he walked past him towards the door.

7

Marco and Vanessa arrived at his cousin's ranch which was situated outside Harrismith, at eleven o'clock. They hadn't spoken much since they left the police station yesterday. He quickly introduced her to Frank and Rhea.

"Follow me," Rhea said to her. They walked down the hall and entered a bedroom. "This will be yours from now on, Vanessa."

"Thanks," she whispered with her heart pounding like crazy against her ribcage.

Marco entered with her luggage and put it on the bed, then exited in a hurry.

His emotions were running wild when he joined Frank outside again.

"We'll take good care of her." Frank said in a soft, calm voice. He was probably the most together person Marco knew.

"I know." It all felt so unreal. He turned his face away from Frank so he would not see the fear in his eyes. Knowing she would be safe with them, eased none of his concerns.

Vanessa appeared behind them. "Rhea sent me to call you. Lunch is ready."

Her sudden appearance startled him; he did not hear her walking up to them.

It was Frank who responded. "Coming."

She went back inside without saying another word.

Marco looked at her as she walked away, following every sway of her body.

It did not escape Frank's attention. For a brief moment his mouth hinted a smile. He moved in closer to Marco. "You weren't supposed to fall in love with her."

Ice-cold adrenalin surged through Marco's veins. He tried to remain as calm as possible. "I did not. The only reason I'm doing this, is because it's my fault she's in this mess in the first place. I'm overwhelmed with guilt. I could have prevented all of this, but I was careless, too sure of myself. I owe her at least this. All I'm doing, is trying to buy her some time, until I can come up with a more permanent solution."

Frank squinted his eyes as he listened to Marco talking a little bit more panicky than he realized. He placed his hand on his shoulder. "You really don't have to pretend in my presence, you are family, and my best friend. I know you well enough to know that you have fallen in love with her, and there is nothing wrong with falling in love."

He was totally caught off guard. "She can never find out, you hear me! No one must ever know this."

"Why not? Why can't *she* know at least? You might just find out that she loves you too."

"She doesn't even remember me. How will she know if she loves me?" Without waiting for a response, he continued, "Please, Frank, don't tell anyone about this. It will only put her in more danger than she already is."

"Sure, I won't tell."

"Thanks, and ... I know you won't talk, that's why I brought her to you. You are the only person I can trust her life with." If only he could stay here with her, but that would create suspicion. Colonel Payne would be onto them in the blink of an eye.

"Come on, the food is getting cold, and I'd bet Rhea's patience too," Frank said and went inside.

Later that evening Marco took Vanessa to the small private lounge adjacent to her room.

He closed the door thoroughly, then went and sat down next to her and took both of her hands. "I know you don't understand why I must leave you here for a while, but Frank and Rhea are the only people I can trust."

He was right, she did not understand. "I know you probably think that since I cannot remember much, I'm stupid, but I am not."

"I don't think you are stupid; how can you even think that?"

"If you would only tell me what is going on, I'll understand. It's humiliating to be treated as a child."

He could not understand why she had to be kidnapped before he realized that he actually loved her. Since her return, he had often wondered if things would have been different if he had realized it before that fateful day. He pursed his lips, then said, "There are major things at work here and I don't have the authority, or the power to tell you." A small pause. "Please, Vanessa, I need you to trust me."

"I trust you."

He let go of her hands, removed something from his pocket and handed it to her. "From this moment on, you are no longer Vanessa Vincent, here is your new identity."

She stared at the envelope. If she was confused before, she was even more so now. "But why?"

"You are now Jennifer Burton," he spoke as if he did not hear her question. Upon seeing that she wanted to say something again, he continued fast, "You have until morning to memorize all of the details in those documents, by heart. You must become Jennifer. From now on you don't respond to Vanessa, Vanessa does not exist anymore, she is dead."

A short silence ensued, then he continued, "Listen, no one else knows about this except you, me, Frank and Rhea. I created this identity all on my own."

"So, they know what's going on?"

"I only told them that you need a place to stay for the time being and that it was essential that I changed your name, that's all they know. Here." He handed her another envelope containing some details about her new life, where she went to school; her old friends; what she did for a living after school;

who she was as Jennifer. "This is everything you need to know... Oh and once you have memorized all of that, burn it. Do you understand?"

"No, I don't understand, but because you're my husband, I will do as you ask."

"Thank you, Jennifer." He addressed her by her new name for the first time. He had worked all night, last night, to create the necessary documents and to do the required preparations. He was glad he had acted upon the idea that popped into his head out of the blue. Creating a new identity was surely a brilliant idea and no one at work knew about Frank or where he lived. She would definitely be safe here until he sent her away to some place more permanent.

He got out of bed the next morning before sunrise. He had not slept at all. He never expected to find himself in a situation even close to the one he found himself in right now.

"Oh, it's you," said Frank when he exited the house and found Marco on the porch.

He wiped the tears from his cheeks as quickly and unnoticeably as possible. "Hey, Frank."

"Why are you up this early?" A long yawn almost cut the question short. "You even beat me to it."

Marco did not answer, only shook his head. "I know I've asked you this already, but it is of vital importance that you don't let anyone near Jennifer, don't trust anyone else but me. No one!"

"I won't. You can trust me."

"Thank you." He had told Frank earlier that her life was in danger, that there were people who wanted her dead. Powerful people. And for that reason, her name had to be changed. He did not give any more detail and luckily Frank did not insist on any.

"I'm leaving after breakfast," he continued after a short silence. "And remember, don't call me unless it is an emergency. I will call you as soon as everything is sorted out."

"Of course."

After breakfast he thanked Rhea for her hospitality; said goodbye and drove off.

Jennifer stood motionless in the same spot for a while after his vehicle disappeared and wondered when she would see him again. Then the realization set in that she had just seen Marco Vincent for the last time. Her husband had thrown her away and left for good, without even explaining why.

She turned around, ran into the house and fell on her bed, crying.

"Leave her. She needs time to work through all of this." Rhea quickly stopped Frank when it seemed as if he wanted to follow her.

"Very well." He turned around and walked away from the house.

He and Rhea were the only family members who knew what Marco's real occupation was. They were the only ones who knew what was going on in his life, except for his best friend, Hein, of course, who also knew. Marco had warned him and Rhea in advance that Vanessa would probably not recognize them. Frank then suggested that they should not try and convince her that she knew them well, because she was going to be uncomfortable as things were. It would be best for her to become acquainted with them afresh; form a new opinion on them, her own opinion. It might even help her regain her memory.

Consequently, he and Rhea knew the truth about their marriage too, as did Hein and his wife, Annie. The four of them were the only ones who knew.

While Marco tried his best to pretend at first, he instantly knew that Marco had fallen in love with Vanessa. He could not understand why Marco refused to tell her. The words slipped out of his mouth, almost inaudibly, "You are in deep, pal. How will you get yourself out of this one?"

Though he knew that Marco and Vanessa were undercover detectives and that their lives were constantly in danger, something about Marco's behavior bothered him. He almost got the impression that Marco was terrified ... and he had never seen Marco scared at anything or anyone, ever!

8

"Colonel Payne wants you in her office immediately," Payne's assistant, Doreen, told Marco when he arrived back at the station.

Reluctant to be there at all, he pursed his lips, walked to the door and knocked once, then entered without waiting for her response.

"Is it done?" She barely looked up from her paperwork. As usual, she did not greet.

"It's done." He tried his best to make those two words sound as convincing as necessary for her to believe him.

She turned her attention to him and made eye contact. The expression on her face made him think he was not convincing enough. He started to panic. Did she know? How?

He did not break eye contact though, but continued to give his best performance. Not only was he brilliant at undercover operations, he was an exceptional actor too, but her demeanor made him doubt in his acting skills today.

At last, she nodded her head. "It's for the good of the company." Her most favorite sentence by far. Not in the least sympathetically towards Vanessa whom she believed died, or towards *him* who had orders to do the deed either.

"Will that be all?" He had enough of her unfair and unreasonable ways. The importance of her opinion of him, was no longer relevant. He had lost everything important to him, and *she* had taken it away!

"That will be all." And just like that, her paperwork had all her attention again.

When he reached the door, her voice forced him to a halt. "Oh yes, one other thing, you are removed from the case, with immediate effect."

This instantly triggered him. It took him a few seconds to calm down before he slowly turned around. "Why? I have completed every single task you've given me without mistake."

It almost appeared as if she found pleasure in his agony and despair. "I don't have to explain anything to you. Hall is taking over the case."

His heart missed a beat. "Hall?"

"Yes. Hall. Is there something wrong with your ears?" She sounded quite annoyed. "Now, go!"

He left the office, not only furious at her for removing him from the case but also extremely suspicious of her assigning Hall. Was she part of this? How much deeper and higher up in the Police Force did this go? How many more officers were involved? Up to what rank?

Highly upset he went for a walk outside. He could not think straight. The whole shebang was rather too much to wrap his head around.

When he finally entered his office, he noticed the envelope dead center on his desk. Inside was a notice that he had been suspended from all field work and that he only had clearance for office work, effective immediately.

He rushed to Payne's office and barged in without knocking. "What is the meaning of this?" Waving the document and envelope in the air. Not even Doreen could stop him before he entered, however she tried.

Slowly she turned her eyes towards him. "So today, it seems you are not only deaf but slow of understanding too."

"What have I done to deserve this, Colonel?!"

"Get yourself under control, Vincent."

"My work is flawless, by the book. This is outrageous."

She got up, turned her back on him and said nothing for a while. This was very unlike her. She never turned her back on a fight. Eventually she turned back and looked at him again. "The decision is final. If you can prove to me that you are capable of following direct orders, I might reconsider your position."

Only when he regained control of his emotions, he spoke, "Yes, Colonel," then left in a hurry before he said something that could get him fired. It was bad enough as it was already.

Marco was chained to his desk, or that was how he experienced it. There was no way he could escape from work early without being seen. He would much rather have taken the day off; he did not accomplish anything anyway.

At last, the day came to an end and he arrived home. He wandered around in his house aimlessly. Walking from one room to the other without doing anything in particular. He thought about Jennifer. He missed her tremendously, but he dared not call her. She would not contact him either, because he had told her not to. Besides, he had taken her cell phone before he left Frank's place. She had been highly upset, he could tell, but she did not object. She had only stared at him with a lost expression in her eyes, and that made him feel even worse about everything.

The bell at the gate rang and brought his mind back to his immediate surroundings. He quickly opened it with the remote control.

"Oh, hello, Hein, Annie. Come in," he said somewhat surprised to see what time it was already.

Marco and Hein had been friends since school. Back then, they got themselves into a lot of trouble because of their vivid imaginations. They had so much fun; so many good memories. Their friendship continued way past school and as a result of their friendship, Vanessa and Annie had become friends too.

"Where is Vanessa?" Annie peeked over Marco's shoulder into an empty house. Marco had told them the good news that she had been found via a voice note on the day they arrived in Botswana for their annual leave. They only returned today.

For a brief moment he considered telling the truth, but managed to stop himself in time. Vanessa's safety was his number one priority. If as much as one more person knew she was alive, the possibility that Payne could find out he had disobeyed her direct order, increased significantly. He trusted Hein and Annie completely, but it was best they did not know; for their own safety as well.

He knew the drill. If Payne got even the smallest whiff that Vanessa was alive, she would brutally interrogate any person who knew him and Vanessa. She would target their family, friends, friends of friends and anyone who might have crossed their paths, until she got to the truth. If that ever happened, they would not be in a situation where they had to try and lie to the best interrogator he had ever met. Her methods were surely illegal and incredibly cruel.

"Vanessa ... died." He felt guilty about the lie, but then, Vanessa *was* dead; Jennifer, on the other hand, was alive and well, but they did not need to know that.

Annie burst into tears. "No! What happened? When? Why haven't you told us?"

Tears made their way down his cheeks too; he didn't even have to pretend to be heartbroken. He knew he would never see her again. Or maybe one last time, as soon as he had figured out how to get her away safely. Far away. The only way to protect her, was to cut all ties.

"She had an accident this morning. I was going to tell you tonight."

Hein, equally as shocked as his wife, was left speechless. After a few seconds of silence, he managed to talk again. "I'm so sorry for your loss, old friend."

"Thank you."

"When is her funeral?"

"Hein! This is way too soon for Marco to have set a date already," Annie replied upset.

Marco gave her a faint smile. "There will only be a service in her honor, the day after tomorrow, since she had requested some time ago to be cremated when she passed away someday." He intended to tell this white lie to everybody who asked, so that her supposed body could never be exhumed to be examined and revealed that it was not her.

He continued, "And there will be no viewing of her body either, which was also her request, as she had no other family except me. She said that people should remember her the way she was. And I am going to respect her wishes."

Annie nodded her head. "Yes, I remember she told me her parents had died a few years ago and that she was an only child."

"Exactly."

The sad news had put a damper on the evening, and Hein and Annie left soon after they finished their first drinks.

* * * * * * * * * *

Dwayne and Pedro were busy reorganizing their studio.

Several days had passed since they submitted the production they had to assemble from old footage. Ever since, they continuously discussed new ideas for the next season, but until now, hadn't come up with anything they both agreed on.

Dwayne sighed heavily. "We'll need to do something drastically different and amazing in order to get the viewers back whom we are about to lose when this poor episode airs."

"Yea, but what, mate? We've been brainstorming for days already, without any success."

"I know! I have a few new, loose ideas."

"I'm listening."

"Perhaps we should change our approach, and focus on one species of marine life each season instead of the broad area-based content of shipwrecks and other so-called treasures. Or perhaps we can take, for instance, all the different types of jelly fish and do an in-depth comparison of them, spanning ... I don't know, maybe three episodes. Then we move on to, for example, all the star fish, then whale types, or whatever. You get the idea."

Pedro considered the idea thoroughly. "That is exactly what we did not want to do, because there are so many other shows doing it already."

"I know, but if you think about it, the viewers love that kind of shows."

"True. What are the other ideas? You mentioned you had a few new ones."

"I was considering doing something with the rocks and beaches, but I don't like that idea anymore. Every time I set foot on the beach; I remember finding Vanessa in the shallow water. Time and again it gives me the chills. I don't think I'll be able to create an exceptional production which includes any beach at all."

"Yea, I agree."

"I wonder how Vanessa is doing?"

"If you ever just listen to me, and call the number I got from Terry, you'd know. Easy as that, mate."

"How will it look if I call a married woman, whose husband forbade me to make any contact?"

Pedro threw his hands into the air and rolled his eyes. "You know, not a day goes by without you mentioning her name, or talking about something we did when she was with us, or about something she said. You ask me almost every single day how I think she's doing, yet you refuse to ask *her*! You are driving me insane, Dwayne. Just pick up the phone and call her! Or even better, mate, go and visit her. We are not busy with anything important right now. We don't even have a clue what to film yet, so nothing is holding you back."

"I can't! She is married, and I will be married soon." Although, he was not entirely sure about him being married soon; things between him and Benice were quite awkward lately...

A soft groan escaped Pedro's lips. "There is nothing wrong with having contact with her, you saved her life, Dwayne. It is normal to show interest in her well-being. It's nothing to do with either of your marital statuses."

Dwayne glared at Pedro for an uncomfortable period of time, clenching his lips together, then reacted, "How long will it be before you get it in your head that Marco told me that I may not contact her?" He turned around and walked out, without even waiting for his partner's response.

Pedro narrowed his eyes as he watched Dwayne disappear through the door.

* * * * * * * * * *

An unpleasant feeling of loneliness and rejection filled Jennifer when she woke up at about four o'clock on her first morning at the farm without Marco. Her new home; Marco had made that crystal clear. Unwillingly she unpacked her suitcases and got dressed in something suitable for the farm life. Yesterday, she was in no mood to unpack, besides, she had no energy either. She had no idea how to adopt to her new life. Last night, her thoughts had run wildly back and forth, almost driving her over the edge.

She had trouble breathing, then instantly decided she would do as many tasks as possible, so she wouldn't have too much time on hand to think about everything.

Daylight had not yet fully broken, but she went outside, determined to find any work she would be able to manage. One of the farm workers taught her how to milk the cows, and she actually enjoyed it.

After that, she went inside and helped Rhea in the kitchen.

Breakfast was served, then she went outside again and asked some of the other farm workers if they perhaps needed assistance.

The day flow by and at nightfall she went for a jog, returned home and fell on her bed, too tired for anything else.

A few days later, after dinner, Frank went and sat with her.

"Are you enjoying it here?"

She smiled. "Yes, I am, it is completely different from city life." The hard manual work was very exhausting, but she was actually happier than she was before she came here – perhaps it was the physical work outside and the calming voices of nature that kept her together. She also did not feel as pressured to remember her past here, even though she continued trying to.

"It is totally different, yes," he responded, also smiling, then asked with a cautious tone in his voice, "Have you perhaps remembered anything yet?"

She stared into the distance for quite some time, attempting to surface any new memory, then she looked at him again. "Nope. The only memory I have, is from after I regained consciousness in hospital." Marco told her not to tell anyone about her attack, so she did not tell Frank about her only memory from before. But because she was not allowed to confide in anyone, not even Rhea, she felt even more lonely and isolated as the day she arrived.

"It must be quite frustrating."

"It is. You know, I literally spent hours every single day to think and all I get are headaches." She struggled to keep her emotions at bay. No matter how hard she worked or how busy she kept herself; she could not free her mind from overthinking.

"Just be patient, Jennifer, don't try so hard, your memory will return at the right time, you'll see."

She nodded, but did not respond.

"I do not want to tell you what you may and may not do, but I wouldn't recommend jogging after sunset."

"Why not? I like jogging after sunset when it is cooler."

"That's understandable, but it can be dangerous. There are currently so many senseless attacks on farmers and people living on farms, it's actually scary."

She sighed. "Okay, I'll do it earlier, before sundown." She hesitated for a moment. "Would you mind giving me something to do? I enjoy milking the cows and doing small tasks for the staff and helping Rhea in the house, but I feel unfulfilled. I would like to do more than only that."

"Very well, I'll show you everything that needs to be done tomorrow morning, then you can decide for yourself what it is you want to do."

"Oh, thank you!"

She was up and awake bright and early the next morning. Frank took her on a tour of the farm and explained every little detail of everything that needed to be done.

They walked past a barn and she saw the tractor inside. "Will you teach me how to drive that?"

He laughed. "Of course."

They continued walking and passed another building which looked like a smaller storeroom, but this one was locked with a heavy steel door.

"What do you keep in here?"

"This is my office. I do all of my planning, orders and bookkeeping in here, where I cannot be disturbed."

"Isn't the storeroom very cold during winter time?"

"It used to be, but since I've put in a nice thick carpet and heater, it's actually quite cozy."

"I see."

"I'll give you your first driver's lesson tomorrow morning after breakfast."

"Thanks! I can't wait."

9

Hein visited Marco after work and they went and sat outside, next to the pool.

"I can't believe Vanessa's gone forever. I feel so sorry for you. It must be extremely hard to come to terms with her passing."

"It is, but I haven't told you everything yet."

"What more is there to tell?" He sounded surprised, almost stunned, that there was information Marco had withheld until now.

"When I informed you earlier that Vanessa was found, I did not give all the detail, because I did not want to upset you while you were on vacation. The plan was to tell you when you were back, but then she passed away before I could tell you about it."

Hein shook his head. "What are you talking about?"

He hesitated for a brief moment. "When Vanessa disappeared, she somehow ended up in Mossel Bay, went for a swim in the ocean and almost drowned." It was not his intention to tell Dwayne's version of the events, but he dared not tell Hein the whole truth either, because it would only be a burden on him and put him in danger too. What did it matter how she landed in the water anyway?

"That's tragic! How did she end up in Mossel Bay? Did she say?"

"No, she didn't … couldn't … because she suffered from amnesia because of the tragedy. She did not even remember her own name, or me, or where she lived. That was the reason she was missing for six weeks."

"Wow! I can only imagine how extremely difficult that must have been for both of you. How did she find her way back?"

He shrugged. "Apparently, some old friend from school recognized her and that's how she found out what her name was. Then a private investigator helped her trace her address."

"I don't even know what to say, Marco. You are so lucky that an old friend recognized her and that she was able to return home before she …" he instantly stopped talking.

Marco gazed into the distance for a few seconds. "Yes. It's a pity she never regained her memory …. and because of that, she didn't allow me to touch her at all."

Hein nodded his head slowly. "I have known for quite some time that you had fallen in love with her. Have you at least told her you loved her before she was involved in that tragic accident?"

Anxiety flooded his mind. If his love for Vanessa was so obvious to Hein and Frank, who else knew about it? If the people from work knew, it could only predict trouble.

"No, I did not tell her. It would only have made her feel uncomfortable. She knew we were married. Since she could not remember the reason for our marriage, it must have crossed her mind that I love her."

"Not necessarily. You should have told her."

He pursed his lips. "Well, I haven't, and now it is too late."

"I'm really sorry you have to go through this, Marco." He got up. "I have to go now, but I'll see you next week, same time, same place."

* * * * * * * * * *

Dwayne and Pedro finally agreed on a theme for the next season of their TV-show and were off to start filming in Cape Town, where they filmed when May (as she was known back then) accompanied them. The main idea was to get more or less the same footage again, but with the new theme in mind.

Back in the owner's cabin, Dwayne edited the footage they shot during that day.

"Oh, how I miss Vanessa's input now," he murmured.

Pedro smiled teasingly. "Sure!"

"What is that supposed to mean?"

"Don't act so innocent, you know exactly what it means, mate."

He pursed his lips, of course he knew what Pedro was referring to, but the bloke tended to forget he was engaged. But then, to be honest, he missed Vanessa way more than what would be considered normal, like Pedro implied. He couldn't stop thinking about her, she was always on his mind.

"Okay, you are right," he admitted at last. "I miss her, not only her input."

"See, now that wasn't so difficult, was it?"

"It was way more difficult than you think, Pedro. Being engaged to Bernice but missing Vanessa isn't quite faithful, is it?"

"Faithful? Did you not say, the other day, that you suspect Bernice of lying and hiding things from you, perhaps seeing someone else, and that you don't trust her anymore?"

"I did, but that doesn't give me permission to do the same."

"Oh, but you don't, mate. You have not even once acted on your desire to see Vanessa and to talk to her, even when I encourage you to."

A heavy sigh escaped his mouth. "Yes, that is true." He turned his head and looked the other way. If Bernice had made any effort to keep their relationship going, his mind would probably not have drifted back to Vanessa so often. It had been weeks now that Bernice ignored him flat-out. No matter how many times he called or how many voice messages he left, she did not reply or call him back. What was he supposed to think of that? This only suggested that she did not have feelings for him anymore. And to be frank, his feelings for her had faded considerably during the past weeks.

Pedro's joyful voice interrupted his thoughts. "Let's go sit outside and enjoy a drink. We're done with today's work."

They went and sat outside.

Dwayne's mood changed slowly and by the time he went to bed, he was at peace with himself again.

The week on the ocean came to an end much faster than Dwayne wanted it to. They headed back home where they finalized everything and submitted the final product without any delays or snags this time.

* * * * * * * * * *

Marco had lost all interest in life, and also his passion for his career. But if he did not show up for work, John would be suspicious, which might inspire him to tell Payne that he had become emotionally unstable because of the recent events. If John managed to convince her about this, he would easily get her to believe that he had fallen in love with Vanessa. And then Payne would personally see to it that he was never assigned a case again, or to be more precise, he would lose his job altogether.

So, he forced himself up every morning, dreaded away the day at the office and when he got back home, worked on a foolproof plan to get Jennifer safely abroad.

Time dragged on, nothing at work changed. The only thing Marco was allowed, was to be glued to his desk, doing boring paperwork.

This continued day after day, week after week.

Six slow weeks had now passed since he had left Jennifer in Frank's care. He had no choice but to battle with his emotions alone. He missed her more and more each day. His entire life had come to a standstill. He had his cell phone in his hands, ready to call her countless times, and every time he forced himself to put it down – in fear that his phone was bugged, as he believed it probably was.

It had become a habit for Hein to visit him once a week, every week.

They had been sitting outside next to the pool for the past hour, and he had not heard a single word Hein had said so far.

Hein's voice came as from afar, "That's the problem, and I don't know what to do."

"Sorry, buddy, I missed that last part. What is the problem again?" To be honest, he did not care about Hein's problem at all right now. He had big enough problems of his own and would probably not even be able to give him any good advice.

"This woman at my work, Suzan, is actively spreading lies about me. Last week she called Annie because she deemed it her personal duty to inform Annie of my apparent unholy practices at work. She told Annie I am laundering money from my own firm! To top it all off, it almost looks like Annie believes Suzan and is now mistrusting me." He repeated his entire dilemma with the same emotions and emphasis as the first time.

Marco frowned: "Why would Suzan do that?"

"I don't know! I don't even know how to talk to Annie about this. Every time I try, she shuts me up."

"You can show her all your records, the check book and bank statements to prove your innocence." He reacted in a somewhat irritated way because Hein was making such a big deal from such a small problem.

"That is not the part that upsets me. Isn't she supposed to trust me and take my word over that of an employee? Marco! You are not listening to a word of what I'm saying, again!"

He jerked his head towards his friend. He had actually given up on listening to Hein's minor problem and was thinking about his own, bigger problems. Lately, this burden weighed heavily on his shoulders.

"Marco?"

Marco turned his head again and stared into the distance. When he finally spoke, his voice sounded gravelly, "I had received orders to kill Vanessa ... purely because she was suffering from amnesia."

"What?!" Hein jumped up from his chair. He knew most of Marco's assignments were dangerous, but he did not think for a moment that Marco would ever receive such an outrageous order, let alone agree to it.

"Did you murder her?" Clear judgment reflected in his eyes and echoed through his voice.

Marco leaned forward, elbows on his knees and chin in his hands. Miserable. "I did not do it, though my boss and everyone involved, believe I did."

Hein sank down into his chair. He was speechless. He gaped at his friend in disbelief.

"I changed her name to Jennifer and left her in Frank's care. No one knows about this. ... Although, I'm not entirely sure whether John believes me." He paused for a moment. "I miss her, Hein. I want to hold her in my arms and tell her I love her, even if it's only once."

"What's stopping you? Why don't you call her, or go and visit her at Frank's?"

He shook his head. "It's too risky. If someone listens in on my calls or follows me, her cover would be blown. I have to come up with a solution to get her out of the country without putting her in any more danger than she already is. That is the only way."

In fact, he had recently finalized the plan to get her out safely, but that information was secret. However, he had to wait before he could execute the plan. The dust of recent events needed to settle first. Luckily, he knew she was safe with Frank. And besides, as long as she was on the farm, he felt close to her, even if he did not see her. He knew his plan was flawless, the hardest part was not acting too soon and getting caught.

"I have to go now," Hein's voice interrupted his thoughts.

They got up and walked to Hein's car. Then he turned towards Marco. "Annie is going to be incredibly happy to hear that Vanessa is alive."

Marco gasped sharply when he realized what he had done. He grabbed Hein by the shirt and pushed him against his car. "You will not tell anyone what I have shared with you today! Got it? Not even Annie! You don't know what will happen if the truth gets out, not only to me and her, but to you and Annie too!" Just as swiftly as he had grabbed Hein, he let go of him again.

Hein got such a fright by this sudden aggressive behavior that he jumped into the car before he spoke. "Don't worry, man, I won't tell."

Marco gave a step backwards. "Thanks. You have no idea how important it is that everybody believes she is dead."

Shaken by the fear of almost being attacked, Hein responded as calmly as possible, "Your secret is safe here, don't worry."

For a couple of minutes after Hein had left, Marco did not move at all. He was annoyed at himself for telling Hein and angry at the situation for not being able to talk to the woman he loved. Disappointed because he found absolutely no satisfaction and pleasure in his career anymore. All this, because of one mistake. One single slip-up! He should have trusted his partner's judgement; he should have listened to Vanessa. She was after all an outstanding detective herself. How could he have been so careless? Now, because of his negligence, both their lives had changed irreversibly.

* * * * * * * * *

"Hey, Dwayne!" Lizelle answered the call joyfully.

"Hello, Lizelle. How are you guys doing?" He could not hide the sense of detachment and sounded rather depressed.

"What's wrong?"

He let out a short but intense sigh. "Nothing too serious. It's Bernice, I have my doubts about her. She's been acting so weird lately; she hardly ever talks to me anymore. In fact, I haven't heard from her in ages, she doesn't answer my calls and when she does, she treats me like a child."

"You know how I feel about her. I have this strange feeling that she's going to let you down big time. In fact, that's what I've been saying since the beginning."

"I know, but she is my fiancée and I don't want to break it off just like that, without even trying to resolve the matter. I don't know what to do. I don't even know why her behavior had changed so drastically. Did I perhaps do something wrong?"

"In my experience, the best way to get to the root of any problem is to talk about it face to face. I suggest you pay her a visit and get things straightened out."

He did not quite like her advice. For some reason, he had actually expected she would say everything was fine; that it was some or other woman thing and that Bernice would be herself again soon enough.

"How exactly should I arrange a visit if she doesn't answer any of my calls? It's not like she lives around the corner, you know."

"Sorry, brother, that's the only advice I can give you." She paused. "To be honest, it sounds to me like you already know the answer; you just don't want to accept it. If you were in love with her, you would have found any excuse to visit her, not find any excuse not to. It's in the middle of the school term, chances of her being home is almost a hundred percent."

"I guess so." He deliberately changed the topic, "Henry asked me again last night to move to America permanently, to be with you."

"And will you?" She sounded instantly eager.

"What about my business here? You know I love my work."

"That's true, but if you stay there, we are not going to see much of each other in future."

"Probably, but I don't have any interest in emigrating permanently. That was your dream, not mine." He loved sunny South Africa profoundly.

"I understand. Have you heard from May yet? What's her real name again? Vanessa, isn't it? Has her memory returned?"

"I don't know. We haven't spoken since I took her home, I've told you her husband said..."

"No, Dwayne, if you actually wanted to know, you would have called her, or dropped by, by now. Is this you not caring enough about her well-being?"

"Of course I care about her well-being! Not a day goes by that I don't think about her. Pedro keeps on telling me to call her, but her husband said that I must forget I ever met her. I have no other option but to obey his orders."

"You've never allowed people to tell you what to do in the past, why now all of a sudden?"

"I don't want any more trouble than what I already have. That man is as unreasonable as it gets."

"What more trouble can you get into, dear brother? You saved her life, surely that counts for something. Any reasonable person would want to check up on someone they've saved."

"Do you really think it is normal to check up on her?"

"Yes, Dwayne, I do."

"I'll think about it. Perhaps it won't be a crime to call her."

She burst out laughing. "No, it won't."

He ended his call to his sister, then went to the rocks in front of his house. Perhaps he should follow her advice; drive to Durban and sort things out with

Bernice. He did have some free time on his hands since they were not filming right now. He could even drop by Vanessa's house afterwards ...

* * * * * * * * * *

Jennifer took the tractor and slasher and went to cut the grass on the field Frank had asked her to. She started with this task after breakfast and was finished when lunch was about to be served.

"Can I quickly go and take a shower before we eat, please, Rhea?"

"Of course. We'll wait for you."

Jennifer disappeared into the bathroom and were back after a few minutes. They sat down for lunch. She focused on her food and only responded when spoken to.

"You seem down lately, Jennifer, do you want to talk about it?" Rhea asked when Frank left and they started to clean the kitchen.

"Oh, Rhea, I feel so rejected by Marco's actions, or rather, his lack thereof. Can he really be so busy that he doesn't have any time left to contact me, or to take one weekend off to come and visit me? Surely, he would have made an effort to see me, if he loved me."

"I can only imagine how much you miss him."

She hesitated for a brief moment. "Can I be honest with you?"

"Of course."

"I don't really know how to explain this. ... I am so confused lately."

"How so?"

"I know he is my husband, but I do not miss him that much. I miss the degree of certainty I experienced with him though. I know I must have loved him before, but that is gone now." She turned her head and stared into the distance, then looked back at Rhea. "Do you think that that is perhaps the reason why he tossed me away and dumped me here? Is this his way of punishing me, because I did not allow him to kiss me or have any physical contact? But it did not feel right to do any of those things while I don't have any feelings for him."

After a few moments of silence, Rhea responded. "Only he can answer those questions."

She threw her hands into the air. "When? I am not even allowed to contact him, and he is clearly not going to make any effort to call me."

"I don't know," Rhea whispered.

"You and Frank seem so happy. Why could my marriage not be like that? Why could my husband not love me the way Frank loves you?"

"Marco is not a bad person, Jennifer."

"Perhaps, but I would have preferred him showing his affection, instead of getting rid of me as fast as possible."

"I'm sure he will explain everything as soon as he comes back for you."

"Do you think he is coming back?"

"He promised he would. Just be patient, Jennifer. I know it's been way longer than he initially said, but he probably has a good reason why he has not returned yet."

"Maybe. Will you excuse me? I need to be alone now for a few minutes." She exited and only stopped jogging when she reached the water stream where she sank down onto the grass and burst into tears.

10

A week later Marco was still bound to his desk. His eyes rested on the stack of papers; his mind somewhere else. He had kind of lost track with time and was rather disappointed when he realized earlier that today was only Wednesday. Yet another grey, unproductive day. If only he could find a way to convince Colonel Payne to investigate John in secret, but he had no idea how. She trusted that man far too much. He had made an attempt yesterday again, merely suggesting that there might be a traitor in their midst ... She had chased him out of her office, accusing *him* of being a troublemaker.

He hated every second of being stuck in the office, not allowed to do anything else. On top of that, he was extremely frustrated because he had not figured out yet who the third person was who attempted to end Vanessa's life.

At last, the day came to an end and he arrived home. He sighed discouraged. Would he ever be able to bring John down? That would be extremely satisfying, even if he never found out who the third accomplice was.

He walked into the kitchen and switched on the kettle. While waiting for the water to boil, it dawned on him that it was time to do something about it. He could no longer postpone. John had probably already done irreparable damage. There was no other option than to talk to Payne openly, and if it got him fired, so be it.

He grabbed his cell phone from his pocket and sent the message. "Colonel, I have to speak to you, privately, it is very urgent. Can we meet tomorrow before work somewhere safe and private?"

As he poured the water into his coffee mug, the bell at the gate rang. Without thinking, he pressed the remote control to open it, went to the door, turned the knob and walked out. He immediately recognized Dwayne.

He pursed his lips. Angry. Irritated. What was *he* doing here? Did he not explicitly told him never to come back?

Then he took a deep breath. "Good day, sir, how can I help?"

Oblivious to what Marco was up to, Dwayne greeted, "Hello, Marco."

"Do I know you?"

Dwayne frowned. "Of course you do, I brought Vanessa back home after she went missing."

"Who is Vanessa?"

Dwayne turned his head sideways, not sure if perhaps Marco was toying with him. Marco was after all not a prankster in any way; much rather an enforcer who would ruin other people's lives without hesitation...

"She's your wife, Marco. She almost drowned. I saved her life and brought her back. She had amnesia at the time. Listen, I was in the area and wondering if she is doing okay, and whether she had regained her memory yet. I want to see her quickly and say hello, that's all."

"I am not married, never been. Perhaps you are at the wrong address. I don't even know anyone with the name Vanessa." He did not feel guilty saying those words to Dwayne, because technically, Vanessa did not exist anymore.

"No, I am not at the wrong address! I have it written down, and I remember your face from when we last met."

"You must be mistaken, or perhaps intoxicated, I have never met you. Now, please leave my property, you are trespassing."

Dwayne turned around, went back to his Land Cruiser and left in a hurry. He was highly upset.

Marco followed Dwayne's vehicle with his eyes until he was out of sight. The audacity to show up uninvited like that and then demand to see Vanessa! Did he not get the message the previous time? Was his intervention not severe enough back then when he had arranged for their recordings to be confiscated? If Dwayne came back again, inquiring about Vanessa, it would leave him with no other choice but to intervene again; with harsher consequences this time.

He entered his house, even more on edge than before. What did Dwayne want really? He had waited all this time, made no contact whatsoever and now he cared about Vanessa again. Why now? Did Bernice recruit him to finish what they started? Was he here to gather information for her and John?

Suddenly he felt uncomfortable and nervous. If there was one person he should never underestimate, it's John, because he was not only intelligent, but also extremely sly.

His heartrate skyrocketed when he realized once again that he could not trust anyone anymore. Not even Hein, because, yesterday, Hein had asked him more than once if Vanessa's memory loss was a lie too, like her so-called death. And if she truly remembered nothing *because that seems unlikely.* Then Hein had asked if she perhaps told him how she disappeared, what happened that she almost drowned, and all sorts of questions. When he answered, it appeared as if Hein did not believe a word he said. Then, out of the blue, Hein asked whether Vanessa had perhaps said something irrational before he took her to Frank's.

Before yesterday Hein did not seem too interested in Vanessa's affairs, only the normal amount of attention which was nothing to worry about. But now, he was highly suspicious of Hein's motive. Why would he be so interested in her, all of a sudden? What did he think she said; and why assume that it would be something irrational? Was it truly only a coincidence that Dwayne showed up the day after Hein interrogated him?

His heart missed two beats. A feeling of powerlessness overwhelmed him. Anxiety flowed through his body as he became paranoid. He had told Hein so many secrets...

He removed the plate with his food which Joanna left in the microwave oven and emptied it in the garbage bin. He did not even have an appetite anymore.

* * * * * * * * * *

At about half past eight on that same evening, a commotion broke out on the farm. The dogs barked aggressively and even the geese were unsettled. Then a male voice spoke to the animals, but his words could not be heard from inside the house.

Equipped with his firearm, Frank headed for the door. "I'll check it out."

Rhea and Jennifer peeped through the windows to see if they could perhaps see anything.

A loud knock at the front door vibrated through the house before Frank could even reach it.

"Who is it?" He called out without opening.

"My name is Dwayne Foster."

A sudden desire to run to the door and open it herself, flashed through Jennifer, but she contained herself since Frank had told her not to trust anyone, especially those she was familiar with.

"What do you want? Why are you on my property this late?" Frank tried his best to sound intimidating.

"My Cruiser has broken down. I am looking for assistance, please."

Frank opened the door slightly, ready to defend himself and his family if necessary. The man appeared well-groomed. He tucked his firearm in the back of his pants, then opened the door completely. "Come in."

The moment Dwayne entered he saw her.

"Vanessa!" He was not only stunned, but overwhelmed with joy at the same time. "What are you doing here?" He suppressed the urge to run the few steps to her and take her in his arms.

Frank quickly glanced at Rhea.

"My name is Jennifer."

"Jennifer?" he repeated, frowning.

Frank stepped in between them. "You said you needed assistance with your vehicle? Come, show me where it is."

Jennifer followed Dwayne with her eyes as he left the house with Frank. She had not heard a single word from Marco since the day he left her here. He had taken her cell phone and said that he was going to destroy it, to ensure no one could ever find her or recover any data from it. There were no words to describe exactly how rejected and isolated she felt because of that. And now Dwayne showed up! She could not even begin to describe how delighted she was to see him. He was the one who stayed by her side when she needed someone the most. He had never once made her feel rejected or lonely.

During the short time she and Marco spent together after Dwayne had brought her back, she had slowly warmed up to Marco, even started to like him. Thus, she not only became desperate to get her memory back, but also to recover the love she was supposed to feel for her husband. She knew she must have loved him before she lost her memory, but she had no feelings for him now.

By midnight, Dwayne's Cruiser was still not fixed. Frank towed it into the yard and left it next to the outbuilding where all his other vehicles were parked, then asked, "Aren't you one of the presenters of that TV-show *Know your coastline – along the deep sea?*"

"I am."

"I knew your voice and name sounded familiar, but I was struggling to put my finger on it this entire time. I'll have a look at your Cruiser tomorrow morning, again. You're welcome to use one of the guest rooms for the night." With that said, he quickly showed Dwayne which room he could use, then went straight to bed.

Dwayne got into his bed too, but did not sleep much at all.

11

Dwayne took a seat across from Jennifer at breakfast. He could not take his eyes off her. He smiled, pleased to see that some of the color had returned to her cheeks. She had been extremely pale last night; he was quite worried about her.

She smiled back at him with sparkling eyes.

Frank interrupted their nonverbal conversation. "We'll go and have a look at your vehicle immediately after breakfast."

Dwayne turned towards him. "Thanks. I truly appreciate your hospitality and help with my Cruiser."

Rhea nodded her head. "Frank often does maintenance and repair work on our vehicles and farm implements. He has a good overall knowledge of engines."

"It is because the farm is situated far from town that I have to try and fix our vehicles myself first. I only call in help from experts when I have done everything I could, and was not successful. Your Cruiser should be in working condition by this afternoon."

Dwayne quickly glanced at Jennifer, then back at Frank. "Thank you."

After the men left to go and work on the Cruiser, Rhea turned to Jennifer. "How do you and Dwayne know each other?"

"He saved me from drowning months ago. If it wasn't for him, I wouldn't be alive today."

Her eyes widened. "Marco told us about the incident, but he failed to mention that it was a famous person who rescued you."

"I'm not surprised; there are actually very few things Marco ever talks about."

"That's true."

* * * * * * * * * *

Marco let out a sigh of relieve when Colonel Payne actually pitched up for the private meeting which he had requested yesterday afternoon.

She sounded a little bit worried, "Want's wrong?"

He took a deep breath before replying. "It's about Hall, Colonel."

Her face turned red from anger, but he carried on swiftly, "Please, just listen to me. I have a very strong suspicion that he is directly involved in the case Vanessa and I were working on before you took me off it."

"Do you have any idea what the impact of these allegations could be on you, Vincent? He is a higher-ranking officer than you are, and a very good detective."

"I know he is, and I also know he is honest and respectable in your eyes, but I've worked for this department for many years as well, and I need you to trust me too. You have assigned me to this project more than a year and a half ago. I've been infiltrating this market under such secrecy that no one in our department, other than you and Vanessa, knew what I was doing. Not even Hall knew about the case. You insisted that he was also left in the dark about it, remember? Well, one of my informants told me that he is not only involved, but possibly the main link between South Africa and the East."

She glared at him in disbelief. "And who is this so-called informant of yours, that you take his word as law without even investigating the matter?"

"You know I will never reveal my informants' names, ever. But you took away my authority and my hands are tied. That is why I arranged this meeting, Colonel, so that this matter can be investigated properly. All I ask, is that you monitor his calls for a start, see if you can find anything suspicious."

"You are asking far more than that, Vincent. You are asking that I doubt my partner, who trusts me with his life. You are asking me to question the integrity of the man who has worked expertly by my side for years." She stopped speaking for a few seconds, looked him straight in the eye, then continued, "You know, Vincent, when Hall came to me and asked to remove you from the case, he said two things. One: he assured me that I don't need to worry about that dirty case, he will pick it up and ensure it gets done. The second was a warning: that you, out of anger, desperation and jealousy might come to me with false allegations against him, and he gave me his word that it will all be lies."

"What?!"

His heart was in his throat. The entire situation was instantly more complicated. If he wanted her to pay attention to him, he would need to proceed very carefully.

He took a deep breath, exhaled slowly. "Colonel, how did he even know I was on this particular case when he asked you to take me off it? My guess is that someone in that market, whose trust I was busy gaining, must have spoken to Hall, and he must have realized I was working in secret investigating this matter. How else could he have known? Don't you find it even a little bit strange that he would ask you to remove me from a case he was supposed to have no knowledge of and then nominate himself? Why do you think he then immediately took the precaution of warning you that any allegation I might make against him, will be untrue? He wanted you to distrust me when I bring his possible involvement under your attention. He knew I would find out eventually..."

"That's enough! Your behavior is unprofessional, ungrounded and extremely misguided. The only reason I am standing here and listening to this garbage, is to see if Hall's analysis and description of you is correct. If I hear one more word from your mouth accusing my partner, you are gone. Did I make myself clear, Vincent?"

Left speechless and paralyzed by the futility of his attempt, he could only nod his head.

"Get yourself to the office immediately!" She spun around and walked away.

A burning sensation shot through his chest as it dawned on him that John Hall had just outwitted him.

When he finally sat down behind his desk, he felt miserable, not quite sure whether Payne would perhaps tell John Hall about their conversation. Luckily, he hardly ever spent time with him at all during office hours, and he never see him after work. There was no one left he could trust.

If Colonel Payne did not give the command herself, or at least gave her permission, he could not arrange with anyone to investigate John Hall. Even Captain Brett, whom he had trusted with a private matter once before, would raise his eyebrows if he approached *him* for assistance. His and Captain Brett's friendship came a long way too. Their parents had been friends for as long he could remember, and consequently they became friends as well. They spent numerous school holidays in each other's company as their parents always went on leave together. While they never became best friends, Brett was most definitely his second-best friend. Naturally he had never told him what his and Vanessa's undercover mission was and he didn't insist on knowing at all.

* * * * * * * * *

Dwayne and Frank struggled the entire day to make any progress on his vehicle. Frank became impatient since he was usually pretty quick at finding fault in broken down cars, and repairing them himself.

At sunset Frank finally called it a day. "I'm sorry, Dwayne, but it seems you'll have to stay another night. I'll continue tomorrow with your Cruiser, if you don't mind."

"Oh, that's all right. I don't mind at all."

They washed their hands, went inside the house and after they enjoyed dinner, Dwayne asked Jennifer to go for a walk with him.

Frank immediately interrupted.

"Under no circumstances!"

"Why not?" Dwayne gave Frank a reproachful look. His behavior was nothing less than treating Jennifer as a child.

"It is way too dangerous. ... You can use the lounge next to her room if you want privacy."

Dwayne stopped himself just in time from saying what he really wanted to. He knew instinctively that he had no choice but to submit to Frank's house rules if he wished to spend more time with Jennifer.

"Come, Dwayne." She made a slight movement with her head.

He followed and only spoke once she had closed the door behind them and they sat down on the sofas. "I thought I would never see you again."

"Me too, Dwayne."

"I went by your house yesterday, but ..."

"You went by my house?"

"Yes."

"Why? Marco told you to never go there again."

"I know, but I wanted to speak to you, and then Marco was acting strangely."

"What do you mean?"

"When I asked about your health and whether I could see you, he said that he didn't know anyone with the name Vanessa. He also said that he is not married, actually claimed he had never been married. He also alleged he'd never met me before. He was quite rude indeed." His facial expression made it apparent that he was quite unsettled by Marco's behavior. But what troubled him even more, was bumping into her here, of all the places in the world, and she claimed not to be Vanessa. Had they discovered by any change that she was not Vanessa after all?

He paused for a moment, then continued, frowning. "Why is your name now Jennifer and not Vanessa anymore?"

She had to force herself not to burst into tears. She was not quite sure why, though, but it sent shockwaves through her body to learn Marco was now telling people they were not married, had never been. She regained some of her composure. She felt sorry for Dwayne too, he must be even more confused than she was.

"I don't know what's going on either, Dwayne. I'd been home for merely two weeks when Marco took me to his work one day and said that I used to work there too. Needless to say, because of the amnesia, I couldn't remember working there, neither did I recognize anyone."

She stopped talking for a brief moment and considered whether she should tell him that she had recognized John, one of Bernice's associates, but decided against it. Marco had made it very clear that she must never reveal that information to anyone.

"The next morning, he ordered me to pack my bags, brought me here, and gave me an envelope containing my new identity. He said Vanessa no longer exists. Then he left, and I've never seen him since." Marco had also insisted she never tell *this* information to anyone either, but she was too hurt to keep it to herself. Besides, Dwayne knew her, and she trusted him.

His frown deepened. "One only does something this drastic when you suspect someone's live is at risk. Are you in some kind of danger?"

"No. I don't know." She turned her head and stared into the distance. Maybe Marco believed John might try something while he was at work and she at home, alone. Then why didn't he say so? Well, even if that was true, it didn't explain why he never made contact with her again. If he loved her, nothing would have kept him away. Nothing!

Frank and Rhea sat close to the door in silence and eavesdropped onto Dwayne and Jennifer's entire conversation; not feeling guilty at all, because Marco said they should trust no one. They did consider the possibility that Dwayne was most likely not the person whom she needed protection from, he was after all a famous TV-presenter. Nevertheless, Frank insisted on listening anyway, since it was impossible to be absolutely sure who her real enemy was. Marco made it clear that it might very well be someone she knew.

* * * * * * * * *

Jennifer entered the kitchen and Dwayne asked immediately, "Where did you disappear to so early this morning?"

"I quickly went to help take care of the animals. I do it every morning."

"But that's not a woman's job."

Rhea responded hastily, "It's her self-appointed task. You should see how capable she is behind the wheel of the tractor."

He turned his eyes towards Jennifer. "A woman of many talents."

She smiled. "Rhea has more skills than me. In any case, I wouldn't have known how to do anything if Frank hadn't taught me."

Frank entered and interrupted the conversation. "Let's go and fix that vehicle of yours, Dwayne."

He smiled at Jennifer, then left with Frank.

They only took a break when Rhea called them for lunch, then continued working on the Cruiser.

At about four o'clock Frank gave a step backwards, clearly frustrated. "This is ridiculous! Why can't I fix this? Usually, I'm able to fix my own vehicles quickly and easily."

Dwayne shrugged. "Sorry for not being able to be of greater help, I don't know a lot about engines."

Frank seemed disappointed in himself. "I'll phone tomorrow and arrange for a mechanic from town to come and have a look. I'm sorry I have wasted so much of your precious time."

"That's not necessary, Frank. I am on holiday now and don't mind at all that it takes longer than we initially thought it would. ... Unless, of course, you don't want me here anymore."

"No, we don't mind you being here." He wiped his hands on a towel. "Okay, let's call it a day. We'll take another look at your Cruiser tomorrow."

"Thanks, Frank. ... Are you and Jennifer family, or is she related to Rhea?"

"Neither. I am Marco's cousin."

"Oh, you and Marco are family." This information came as a surprise to him. "Why did he change her name and brought her here and not to her own family?"

"He deemed it necessary. How well do you know Jennifer? Except for saving her life back then, what else do you know about her?"

"I know her real name is Vanessa and that she and Marco are married. I know she suffers from amnesia and that she has difficulty accepting it. Since I arrived here, I also learned that she loves to exercise and that she likes the outdoors way more than being indoors."

"Did you know her before she lost her memory?"

"No, and after I took her home back then, we never saw each other again ... until I arrived here, of course."

* * * * * * * * * *

Giving up was something Marco had never done before and he was not planning on doing it now. John might have defeated him by going to Payne first and won her trust by feeding her lies, but he was not about to surrender. As long as he still had his job, it meant John had not yet convinced her to get rid of him entirely. Which was a good sign. He deduced from this, that she had not told John about their conversation from earlier.

He had no doubts that if John had the slightest suspicion that he knew about his involvement, he would have taken steps by now to have him silenced for good.

He waited impatiently for John to leave the building after his so-called 'tea-break', then he went to Payne's office, approaching her with even greater care than before.

"Colonel, regarding my last case ..."

"I told you yesterday already; I don't want to hear another word about Hall," she interrupted.

"I wasn't going to say anything about him, Colonel."

"Then go on. What about your last case?"

"Has there perhaps been any progress since Hall took over?"

"Yes, he has actually made significant progress in the few days, much more than you and Vanessa had in the year and a half you were investigating." It almost sounded as if she was accusing him and Vanessa of not doing their job, or that they had deliberately dragged their feet.

"Would you care to elaborate, please, Colonel?"

"Why? It's got nothing to do with you anymore."

"I would be a terrible detective if I didn't care about the outcome of a case I was investigating, wouldn't you agree?"

The expression on her face sent shivers down his spine. The look on her face told him that she in fact thought he was a terrible detective, but didn't want to say it out load.

He clenched his jaw for a brief moment to regain his self-control. He was not going to allow her to derail his undertaking. "Don't you find it strange that someone new on the case makes so much progress in such a short period of time? Do you truly trust his results? Because, if I were you, it would have bothered me tremendously."

"Vincent, I'm warning you ..."

"Don't worry, Colonel, I'm not accusing him of anything. You are in charge of this branch and probably know your staff better than anyone else." He spoke with suggestion loaded in his voice, then left her office. All he could hope for now, was that she would think about his words and considered investigating John Hall's sudden interest and almost impossible speedy progress in the case.

* * * * * * * * * *

Dwayne smiled, secretly pleased, when Frank failed to have fixed his Cruiser by the end of the fifth day after it had broken down only a few meters from the entrance to the farm. Luckily, Frank had no idea that he was sabotaging his own vehicle as soon as it became clear that Frank was about to fix it. Although he truly could not fix his Cruiser the other night on his own in the darkness, he actually knew more about engines than he let on. But he would do just about anything to stay as long as possible. He was afraid that if he left and came back later, Jennifer would be gone again. He knew instinctively they would not tell him where they sent her off to this time. He was not going to let that happen. As long as he stayed here, he could keep an eye on her himself.

"Let's sit under this tree," he interrupted his own thoughts, that flashed through his mind while he and Jennifer were walking outside.

"I don't think Marco loves me anymore," she said abruptly, but sounded detached.

"Why so?" He, on the other hand, was thrilled about this news.

"Because he never even once made contact with me since he left me here. How can my own husband simply drop me here and then never return? I think ... it was his plan from the start to dump me here like trash. If he loved me, he would have come back for me by now, or called to talk to me at least."

Her words only confirmed his own suspicions that Marco did not love her anymore. Maybe this was his strategy to persuade her into an easy divorce agreement. Clearly Marco had no intention to save their marriage. But why? Had he perhaps gotten so frustrated with her condition that he could not stand her anymore? Or had he met someone else – while she was missing, or even after she returned and he had to face the reality that she could not even remember him?

"I'm so sorry, Jennifer. It must be devastating to be treated like this by your loved one."

She sighed, then shook her head. "The fact that my husband treats me like this, is hurtful, yes, but strangely enough, I don't have any feelings for him. I must have loved him once, or else we wouldn't have gotten married in the first place. This is so confusing, Dwayne. I feel completely humiliated because Marco could get rid of me so quickly, but ... I am not heartbroken at all."

"Jennifer …" he whispered. "If only there was something I could do to make things easier for you."

A faint smile touched her lips. "Thank you, Dwayne."

* * * * * * * * *

"It appears my Cruiser has bigger problems than I thought. I should have traded her for a younger model before I started my journey," Dwayne said the following afternoon when Frank was clearly frustrated with himself as well as the vehicle he could not fix.

Frank shook his head, annoyed. "Your Cruiser could have been fixed ages ago already if you only let me call out a mechanic."

"I'm in no hurry; I am on vacation now, I've told you. But I appreciate your help. Let's call it a day, what do you say, Frank?"

"Fine."

"Thank you." He rushed to the house and took a quick shower, eager to spent the rest of the afternoon alone with Jennifer. Earlier today, shortly after lunch, he had asked Rhea to pack a picnic basket and also a blanket, so he could take Jennifer on a picnic.

"Let's go," he told Jennifer and the two of them set off.

They made themselves comfortable at the stream, completely oblivious that their every move was being watched closely.

Frank and Rhea were standing at the window, observing Dwayne and Jennifer through binoculars.

"Frank?"

"Yes, dear?"

"Do you also get the impression that he is not really eager to leave?"

"It would appear so, yes." He put the binoculars on the windowsill and rubbed his eyes. He had noticed that Dwayne was fiddling with the Cruiser's engine the day before yesterday already. He did not say anything because he thought that the guy was probably only trying to help in his own inexperienced way. But now he could not help but wonder if perhaps Dwayne was deliberately sabotaging his vehicle. He took the binoculars and pressed it against his eyes again.

They sat on the blanket for a few minutes, talking about the beautiful trees and flowers at the stream, then Jennifer lay down comfortably on her back.

Dwayne rested his weight on his side and on one arm so he could lie down beside her but still see her face. He gently stoked her cheek with the colorful feather he had picked up on the way to the stream.

"Close your eyes," he whispered.

The delicate, ticklish touch of the feather on her eyes and lips was absorbing all of the tension and sorrow she had been experiencing ever since she regained her consciousness in hospital.

His voice was as tender as the feather. "Think of the clouds. Imagine them pulling up next to you, and you getting onto them ... Now they float away slowly, taking you to your happy place." He waited a few seconds. "Are you there yet?"

A smile slowly made its way to the corners of her mouth as her mind drifted with his words.

As he stroked her face with the feather, his eyes were just as much touching her closed, pink eyelids; her slightly blushing cheeks; her soft lips ... Slowly he bent down and equally tenderly as the feather, he put his lips on hers.

Without opening her eyes, she responded by accepting the kiss.

Neither of them wanted this kiss to end, so they stretched the moment as long as they could, without making it awkward.

"You know," said Frank, clearly upset by the scene he witnessed, "by the time Marco wakes up, he might have lost his wife." He was obviously uncomfortable with the idea that Jennifer was allowing Dwayne such privileges while being married to his cousin.

"Oh, but you forget one small detail," Rhea said, smiling naughtily.

"What detail?"

"That Marco is married to Vanessa Vincent, not to Jennifer Burton, remember?" Because Frank had not told her that Marco had fallen in love with

Jennifer, she found nothing wrong with this new romance.

He made a soft groaning sound. "They are still the same person, Rhea."

"Perhaps, but it doesn't change the fact that she is no longer Vanessa. Vanessa is dead. Jennifer is alive, and she is unmarried. Did you not read the papers Marco left?"

"Off course I've read them." He put the binoculars down and went to his room. If Marco hadn't forbidden him to tell anyone about his affection for her, he would have walked out there and chased Dwayne away right now.

Jennifer was getting lost in Dwayne's feathery kiss on her cloud at her happy place.

Then she opened her eyes, pushed him away and raised herself to a sitting position. She seemed completely lost.

"What's wrong?"

"Nothing," she said frowning. Suddenly, her confusion turned into excitement. "I've got my memory back!"

"That's marvelous!" A billion questions crossed his mind, but he forced himself to keep quiet. Let her work through it first.

The expression on her face changed drastically as yet another memory entered her mind. She turned pale and jumped up. It was not only *her* life that was in danger!

147

"Woah, what now?"

"Nothing." She agitatedly threw everything back into the picnic basket, grabbed it and ran towards the house. John Hall's last words to her, before they threw her overboard, echoed in her mind. *I will find every single person you have ever cared for or loved, and I will bring an end to their lives. So, if you have told anyone about this mission, they will not be able to let any information slip, ever!* He had not taken her seriously when she said nobody knew anything because she had not told anyone. He had only laughed, then shouted that he didn't believe her at all.

Dwayne was completely stunned by her strange behavior. It took a few seconds to realize she was already a couple of meters ahead of him. He grabbed the blanket and started running to catch up. What did she remember? It must be something horrible, because the only other time he had ever seen her like this, was when she saw and recognized Bernice.

Moments before she reached the door, he caught up with her. She stopped, turned towards him and put the basket down.

He threw the blanket next to the basket on the ground and opened his mouth to speak, but she wrapped her arms around his neck.

Automatically his arms encircled her waist and he pulled her closer. The uneasiness in his heart was getting too much to handle when the feeling that something bad was about to happen sneaked up his chest.

Then she kissed him. At first, somewhat hesitant, then more passionate and even more ... she was completely out of breath when she let go of him. "Thank you."

"For what?" He too was breathing heavily.

"For giving me back my memory. ... Now I need you to leave immediately and never come back. Never contact me again, goodbye, Dwayne." With that said, she turned around and went inside. Tears ran down her cheeks.

He was left completely dumbstruck. He wanted to call out to her that this could not be goodbye! But the words stalled in his throat.

* * * * * * * * * *

Marco's heart missed a beat when his cell phone rang and he saw Rhea's name on the screen. Something terrible must have happened, because his orders were clear that they were not allowed to contact him unless it was an emergency.

He expected the worst news ever when he took the call. "Hello, Rhea, what happened?"

"I got my memory back," Jennifer said in a surprisingly formal voice.

Adrenaline surged through his veins; he did not expect to hear *her* voice at all. "That's a relief," he responded, then thought by himself: *Could it not have happened sooner? Before it was necessary for all of these drastic measures?*

He was not ready for her next question, "Why did you disregard a direct order? Why did you not kill me?"

"Can you not figure that out for yourself?" His voice was almost inaudible. His hands were shaking uncontrollably. Without waiting for her response, he rumbled, "You have been my colleague for so long, I couldn't do it. It's too cruel and unreasonable of Payne to expect me to do such an inhumane thing. Purely because she believes you are no longer fit for the operation; doesn't mean you have to be killed."

"What if you get caught?"

"Who is going to find out? No one knows or even suspects that you are alive. Nobody knows your new identity. Not a single person, besides the four of us, knows where you are staying now. For all they know, you were cremated." He neglected to mention that Hein also knew, but that was information she need not know.

"Thanks, Marco, I'll never forget this. The real reason I'm calling, is to tell you I know who was the third person on the yacht."

"I'm listening."

"His name is Buddy Budler." Inside her heart, she was definitely not as calm as her voice sounded. She had never seen Buddy before that day, but she could recall his face and his voice now clearly. She never wanted to experience a day like that ever again. But the memory of that horrifying day was flashing in her mind, over and over again, like waves crashing and retreating on the beach, never-ending.

She took a deep breath, then continued, "When I went with Bernice to meet her superiors, John was there, and when he saw me, he quickly gave the order to grab me and take me to the yacht. They tried everything to find out what I knew, and who was working on the case with me. I told them nothing, and when they made peace with the fact that they would not get any information from me, he gave the order to kill me."

Chills ran down his spine at the memory of how close she had come to dying on that particular day. "Thank you for calling me straight away. I'll see what I can find on this Buddy guy. We'll talk again later." He ended the call and exhaled loudly, overwhelmed by the news, then he contacted Hein.

"She got her memory back!"

"That is great news, Marco. How do you know this?"

"She just called me." Without even thinking about what he was doing, he told Hein everything she had shared with him, then ended the call. Hein had been his anchor since he left Jennifer in Frank's care. His doubts about Hein had faded as the days had passed since he interrogated him the last time he visited. He convinced himself that he was going down the spiral of paranoia and that he should not allow this to influence his judgement or his relationship with his friend.

He put his cell phone down and went to pour himself a cup of coffee. His thoughts jumped back to the time when Colonel Payne became their new commander.

She had called them all for an urgent staff meeting and made them sign a very unusual contract.

He remembered her saying, among other strange 'house rules' she implemented, "It's for the good of the company, and for the good of all squads that you agree to the following: If any of you, for whatever reason, lose your memory, your partner has the explicit duty to end your life, in order to keep every squad, and the information gathered, safe."

When no one wanted to agree to such unlawful demands, she started to threaten them with severe penalties and punishments.

He was truly struck by her heartlessness and persistence to enforce such an obscure clause.

He never understood her argument, but if she really thought someone with amnesia had to be killed, why did it have to be their partner who pulled the trigger? If it truly was for the good of the squad, as she claimed, why not get someone who was not as emotionally attached and close to that person to do it?

Most of the officers signed eventually, but those who refused and resisted, started to disappear one by one over the course of a few weeks following her unreasonable demand. He only signed because he genuinely thought something like that would never happen to him, ever. How wrong he was ...

12

At six o'clock the next morning, Marco's phone rang. He answered drowsily. He had spent the entire night looking for any information on Buddy, but could not find anything, not even on the secret database he had access to.

"The guy you've sent to fetch Jennifer, has left with her moments ago," Frank said in a stern voice.

Marco was now wide awake. As if Frank had thrown a bucket of ice onto his face and chest, his entire body started shaking, his mouth became dry. "Stop kidding around! I didn't send anyone to fetch her."

"But he said he had specific orders to take her to you."

Marco almost had a panic attack. Someone had found out that she was alive, worse yet, where she was hiding. "Nonsense! You're joking, right?"

"No."

"Then who was it?"

"What did he say his name was again?" He could hear Frank was actually talking to himself, then he spoke louder, "Oh yes, now I remember, it's Buddy Budler."

"I expressly told you to trust *no one*, and to let no one near her!"

"I'm sorry, Marco. He really sounded like he knew what was going on and he had information only you could have given him. He gave us no reason not to believe him."

"What have you done?! What car did he drive?"

"A silver BMW."

"Did you get the registration number?"

"No."

"Dammit, Frank!"

"I'm sorry, Marco, I truly thought you sent him. I'll help you to catch the guy, they can't be too far yet."

"No, leave it! From now on, I'll handle things myself. And for heaven's sake, keep quiet about this before the wrong people find out I'm searching for this Buddy guy!" He ended the call abruptly. He was furious.

At a quarter past seven, when Dwayne walked into the kitchen, he immediately enquired where Jennifer was. Because, usually when he arrived, she was already there.

Frank shrugged. "She left quite early this morning."

"Where to?"

"Marco sent someone to take her home." He was in a rather bad mood since he had made the call to Marco. He kept the details to himself, as Marco ordered him to do. "I'm going into town after breakfast, I'll send someone to come and fix your Cruiser, and then I'm going to the bank too."

"I'll come with you ..." Dwayne started talking.

"No, you stay here, if the mechanic arrives while I am in town, you can set him to work. I don't like Rhea being alone here with a bunch of strangers." He walked out and only retuned at about half past eight, just in time for breakfast.

They ate in silence, but no one actually enjoyed the meal. Afterwards Frank disappeared to his room.

"I'll be back in a minute, Dwayne, I'm quickly going to see if he is okay."

"It's fine, Rhea, I'll start cleaning up here in the meantime."

"Thanks." Then she left the kitchen.

Dwayne was almost done with the dishes when Frank left the house and Rhea entered the kitchen again.

"Is everything alright, Rhea? Frank seems quite upset."

"Don't let his attitude bother you. He's upset with Marco because he can be very unreasonable at times. He brought Jennifer here and expected Frank to take full responsibility for her life and safety. He said it would be for a couple of days only, but it's been almost two months now. It takes a toll after a while, you know, being responsible for someone else without an actual end date."

He nodded. "I understand completely."

She smiled faintly. "He is mad at Marco for not notifying him in advance that someone was coming to pick her up this morning. He expected Frank to be responsible, but then *he* goes and does something foolish like this!"

"No wonder Frank is in a bad mood."

"Yes, and to be honest; I think he is somewhat annoyed with you being here too."

"Why?"

"Initially he did not mind your presence since we both saw the positive influence you had on Jennifer. But he did not expect you to stay this long though. Because he was already tense by being responsible for Jennifer, your extended stay only caused him to be even more stressed."

"I'm sorry for that."

"Don't be, I don't mind you staying longer than we initially expected. I couldn't help noticing that you like Jennifer a lot." A small, naughty smile touched her lips.

"Thanks, and yes, I like her a lot."

"Do you know that she is a detective, an undercover agent?"

"What?! No!"

"Yes. She and Marco both. They are partners. ... I am tired of all these lies and secrets, Dwayne. I am not supposed to say anything, but they were never really married. Apparently, they had to pretend to be married for the last case they'd been working together. I don't know why. It was during that investigation she went missing, and you found her in the ocean. Since then, she suffered from amnesia, but this you already know."

Mixed emotions sent electric shock waves through his body. He was extremely relieved to find out that she and Marco were not married after all. Thunderstruck to learn that she was in fact an undercover detective. Angry because Marco took her away again.

* * * * * * * * * *

Jennifer gaped at Buddy in shock while they drove in silence. She could not believe that *he*, of all people, would deceive her and Marco like this.

She finally got herself calm enough to speak. "I have seen many people stabbing each other in the back and betraying one another, but doing it on this scale, and in this way, is cruel, even for you."

He laughed out loud. "If you say so, Sweetheart." Then he laughed again. "You want to know what's cruel, Sweetie? Wait till your husband arrives."

"What makes you think he will show up? He doesn't even know that you've kidnapped me, or where you are taking me to."

His eyes glittered in victory. "Oh, he knows, Sweetheart. He knows. But what he doesn't know, is that we will be ready and waiting for him. You see, we have set a trap, and in his desperate attempt to play the hero, he will run to his death so fast, he won't even know what hit him."

An invisible hand grabbed her at the throat and squeezed the life out of her. Would Marco be clever enough not to walk straight into the trap? Her anxiety faded slightly when she reminded herself that Marco was an extraordinary gifted detective; and one of his specialties was precisely this – to trap very high-ranked criminals. He would surely recognize a trap ...

These thoughts calmed her nerves for a brief moment only, then anxiety set in again. She struggled to keep her composure. "What are you going to do with me?"

"Don't you worry about that, Sweetheart. We won't do too much before Marco arrives. You do not host a show before the audience shows up, now do you?"

She could hardly breathe anymore. The word 'mercy' did not exist in these people's vocabulary. They would do practically anything to ensure their operation remained operative and *their* involvement remained secret. Then it hit her that she and Marco were way over their heads in trouble. These people were cold-blooded murderers, as she had experienced firsthand already. How much more were they willing to do?

She turned her face away from him in an attempt to settle her nerves enough so that she could think straight.

Her mind drifted from the current threat on hand to where it all started. Barely a year and a half ago she and Marco were assigned to this case. They had to infiltrate the market of human trafficking (children, to be exact). They had to determine who was the main link between South Africa and the East. The smuggling of children had increased so drastically that the department needed a more aggressive approach.

To avoid suspicion as to why the two of them suddenly showed an interest in the market simultaneously, they needed to pretend to be married, since this was a much bigger undertaking than one person could possibly handle alone. Colonel Payne changed their identities to Vanessa and Marco Vincent on all of the databases. According to the 'records', they got married three years ago. And because this was a very dangerous case, she had to break all ties with her family too. She did not have any contact with her parents or any of her two siblings during the entire time. They even told Marco's cousin and his best friend she was an only child whose parents had passed away. At first, she thought it was a brilliant idea and that her and Marco's families would be safe no matter what happened. But this false sense of security came tumbling down when John said he was going to hunt her loved ones, because he knew her true identity and who her parents and siblings were. Changing their names did not serve its purpose after all.

Marco introduced her to Frank and Rhea and explained that for their new undercover operation, they needed to be married. Luckily, they did not ask too many questions and immediately accepted her as family. It was a little tougher explaining the matter to Hein and Annie. They asked a lot of questions, questions they were not prepared to answer. Hein's biggest concern was why Marco would need to enter into a marital relationship to do an investigation. It made no sense to him at all. He and Annie did not accept her as easily as Frank and Rhea did, but they eventually warmed to her and they became good friends in the end.

She and Marco studied the schools that had the highest disappearance rates of children within the last few years. They identified the two schools where most children disappeared from. She started working at one of them and Marco at the other one. Their mission was to focus on the organized and orchestrated formal organization of child trafficking rather than the odd snatching of a child at a gas station or shopping center. That part of the case was given to other detectives.

Her first priority was to identify individuals whose personalities and behavior created the suspicion of involvement in human trafficking – both teachers as well as parents. She created a shortlist of potential suspects in need of further investigation. It did not take long before Bernice received a red dot next to her name. She became her number one suspect.

Bernice gave way more attention to the children to be considered normal. She handed them sweets, gifts and other things way too often to be regarded as incentives. She spent a lot of time talking to some children in private. After school she would take some of them, one at a time, for a ride in her car while they waited for their parents.

So, she befriended Bernice deliberately. And as they got to know each other better, she had constantly steered the conversation to smuggling and selling of children, very delicately of course. She once even said to Bernice that it was not the worst thing in this world. Initially, Bernice ignored her comments completely, but as time passed, she paid more attention. One day, as they walked to their classrooms, Bernice said that if she was really interested, she could teach her how to kidnap a child successfully.

That was when she started going to school wired, and recorded everything Bernice taught her. A few months later, she was apparently ready for her first solo task. She had to offer Emily a lift home and deliver her to a specified location. Emily, the beautiful, blonde hair, blue eyed, grade one girl, who missed the bus 'by accident' because she had to 'talk to miss Bernice about her grades after school'.

That night she had trouble sleeping, she was nauseous and sick the entire time. When she finally dozed off, she had nightmares about what the buyers were doing with little Emily, who trusted her to take her home safely.

She begged to be removed from the case, but her request was denied. Marco ensured her that it would get easier with time. But it didn't.

Every child she helped kidnap, haunted her nonstop. She cried herself to sleep every single night. She could not take it anymore.

She remembered every little child's face, their voices, and their last words. They echoed through her mind one by one, night after night, driving her insane. She was so disturbed by this, that she intended to resign from the Force as soon as the case was solved.

The main purpose of this mission – to find out who the sellers of those stolen children were, was finally within reach. They were getting close, really close when she was granted the privilege to meet the man in charge. Bernice told her that she was ready to work on her own; to receive her own line of buyers. According to Bernice, she was good enough and no longer needed her supervision. If only she had known in advance how bad of an idea it was to meet the main man in person...

Buddy's voice ripped her out of memory lane. "It is a shame that things had turned out this way, Sweetheart. It would have been so much better if you hadn't regained your memory. For all of us. I would have left you to live your pitiful life in peace. But now, now the risk is too high."

* * * * * * * * * *

Dwayne wandered around aimlessly, waiting for the mechanic Frank said he would send, to arrive. His thoughts were flying around, frantically. Why would Marco summon Jennifer now, all of a sudden? What exactly did she tell him when she called him yesterday? Why would she go back to him in a heartbeat as if nothing had happened, the moment she regained her memory? His heart sank into his shoes: had she perhaps developed feelings for Marco during their fake marriage?

It was about ten o'clock when a vehicle came speeding up the dirt road towards the house. He secretly hoped that it was not the mechanic; he would not like such a reckless person to touch his vehicle.

It was, however, not the mechanic, but Marco.

Marco was trapped in his own mind. Furious. His heart almost stopped completely when Frank had called him this morning, informing him that Jennifer had left with Buddy. When Jennifer told him yesterday that Buddy was the third person who was on the yacht that crucial day, he was certain he had heard that name before. But he couldn't remember where.

This morning though, while he was preparing to find her before Buddy could completely disappear with her, again, he suddenly knew exactly who Buddy Budler was. Mad at himself for not realizing it sooner, he jumped into his car and sped of. When they were kids, he had always told him that if he was to ever do something sinister or illegal, he would use the name Buddy Budler, then nobody would know it's him; and he would use a BMW as his escape vehicle to be uncatchable.

His entire body was shaking from rage as he grinded to a halt. A cloud of dust surrounded his car.

"What are you doing here?" he yelled at Dwayne, the first person he saw when he threw open his door and got out.

"My Cruiser broke down close by and I ..." By the time he got to 'and', Marco was already gone, clearly not interested in Dwayne's explanation whatsoever.

He rushed into the house, shouting, "Frank! Rhea!"

Rhea ran towards him. "Marco, what are you doing here? Where is Jennifer?"

"Where is Frank?" He yelled, close to a state of panic.

"He went to town," she responded, astounded by the terror in his voice.

"When did he leave?"

She glanced at her wrist watch. "A few minutes after nine. Why? What's going on?"

"We are leaving now. Come!"

"Where are we going? Can't we rather wait until Frank gets back?"

"It will be too late by then! We need to find Jennifer, now!" He grabbed her by the arm and dragged her to his car.

"I'm coming too," said Dwayne, who overheard the entire conversation, since he followed Marco inside. He knew something was wrong when Marco showed up and seemed upset and panicking. He instinctively knew it had something to do with Jennifer, but was absolutely furious to learn that she had apparently disappeared. Again!

Marco had not even finished his answer, "Under no circumstances ..." before Dwayne was in the passenger's seat.

"Come on then, let's go!" Dwayne commanded.

With no time to waste, Marco decided to let Dwayne tag along. He pushed Rhea into the backseat, closed the door, jumped in behind the steering wheel and took off. While driving, he unlocked his phone, opened an application and gave it to Dwayne. "See that red dot? That is the car in which Jennifer is right now. You tell me where to drive."

When Vanessa (as she was known back then) went missing, he felt so powerless that it nearly drove him over the edge. He never wanted to feel that helpless again, so, he installed a tracking device in the cell phones of each one of his closest friends and family members, without their knowledge and consent of course. If any of them were to be kidnapped or got into trouble, he would always be able to find them, and never be that stranded again. He knew with the line of work he was doing, that all of his close friends and family could be in danger at any time. He wanted to be ready for such a day. Now, that day had arrived and he was glad he did install those tracking devises after all.

He sighed, suddenly relieved that Dwayne was there too, glad to have an extra set of eyes while he drove, especially since he had no intention of keeping to the speed limit, or respect any road sign for that matter. Buddy and his partners had already tried to kill her once, they will stop at nothing to succeed in doing it today.

Dwayne responded, highly upset. "Why did you come all this way, the opposite direction of the vehicle Jennifer is in, when you could have saved so much time if you had gone straight for it?"

"I need backup. Do you think I stand a chance against three murderers alone? Because I sure don't think so." He truly hoped that it would only be the three of them who had kidnapped her back then, who would be present, and that they did not call in reinforcements ... or better yet, that it would only be Buddy. But there was no way to tell, so, he needed to be prepared for the worst.

"Murderers?! ... Then step on it! At this rate my grandmother will outrun you!"

Marco, already at top speed, only pursed his lips.

"Why is everybody trying to kill her?"

"Let's explain things when we get her back safely, okay? And here, put this on." As he spoke, he pulled out the disguise he kept under his seats for emergency situations.

Dwayne took the mask and wig from him. "What is this for?"

"You'll find out soon enough."

Rhea was so silent; Dwayne had almost forgotten she was there too.

Her voice was shaky when she finally spoke. "I don't know how I will be of any assistance in saving Jennifer from murderers."

Marco did not even respond to her words.

Dwayne quickly peeked to the backseat. If he had to be honest, he agreed with her. He frowned as the question crossed his mind: Why did Marco insist she came along? Then it dawned on him that Marco went to get Frank's help, and because he was not home, grabbed her as a desperate replacement. He was so panicked; it did not even occur to him that he did not need her anymore when he (Dwayne) offered his help.

They entered a parking lot of a warehouse and pulled in next to the car in which the tracking device was active and sending a signal to Marco's phone. The area seemed abandoned, except for four vehicles, Marco's included.

He grabbed a pen and a piece of paper from the console, wrote down an address and handed it to Dwayne. "Punch this into your phone's GPS. The moment Jennifer is in the car with you, you go as fast as you can to this address. Got it? Come, take the driver's seat."

Marco got out, then opened the back door. "Come, Rhea."

Dwayne frowned troubled. Why would he take Rhea along? Did he actually think she would be better help against murderers than him? He pursed his lips angrily, but got behind the steering wheel, as instructed. Then he noticed that Marco and Rhea were standing outside the warehouse and that Marco was holding a gun against her temple.

Rhea seemed petrified.

"What the hell?" Dwayne shouted out, startled. In his panic, he struggled for a moment to grab hold of the doorhandle, but before he could even open it and get out, Marco's voice echoed loudly through the air.

"Hey, Buddy! I've got a proposition for you! We make a little exchange. My wife, for yours!"

Dwayne's heart almost stopped beating. He jerked his head into the direction Marco was facing. The warehouse door was slightly open, but there was no movement whatsoever and also no response.

He took a deep breath, then shouted again, "I am going to count to three! ... One... Two..." A shot reverberated through the empty parking lot, followed by a terrified scream from Rhea. He had shot her in the foot. Her body almost collapsed, but he was prepared for this; his grip on her was tight enough to keep her standing, gun back at her temple.

Dwayne instinctively ducked down, horrified. He did not expect *this*, even though Marco had told him earlier that Jennifer was in the hands of murderers.

Then he heard Frank's voice echoing, "What are you doing, Maniac!? Why did you have to involve Rhea?"

He quickly got back into a seated position behind the steering wheel, simultaneously looking into the direction where Frank's voice was coming from. There was someone standing in the doorway, but that man looked nothing like Frank. Only when he removed his disguise, did Dwayne recognize him.

Rhea spoke through her tears; her voice reflected the incredible pain she experienced from her wounded foot. "Frank? Is that you? What's going on?"

He only gazed at her, but no words of comfort came from him, in fact, he did not even say one single word to her.

Another man appeared next to Frank, aiming his gun at Marco.

Dwayne could not believe his eyes nor his ears. Why was Frank wearing a disguise; why did Marco call him 'Buddy'; and how the hell did Marco know? His confusion turned into rage. If Marco had known that Frank was a murderer all along, why did he leave Jennifer in his care in the first place? Why did he put her in the lion's den?

"It's easy, Frank," Marco sounded in control of the situation, "you hand over my wife, unharmed, and I'll hand over yours. Also, if you would be so kind as to ask John to put down his gun, or you might receive the corpse of your wife in return for mine. Don't test my reaction time by doing anything funny, you will lose." Marco knew very well how much Frank loved Rhea, and that he would not let any harm came to her if he could prevent it. That was why he went to get her first before he followed them here. She was his bargaining chip.

A tiny, evil smile appeared at the corner of John Hall's mouth; victory was written all over his face. He raised his eyebrows and tightened his grip on his weapon.

Marco was not intimidated by this at all. "Let's try again, shall we? One... Two... Th..."

"Okay, okay! Stop! Don't shoot!" Frank said, then gaped at John. "Lower your weapon! Now!"

When John lowered his arm, Frank turned his head towards the door and called over his shoulder to someone inside, "Bring her here, right away!"

A few seconds passed, then Bernice appeared, holding Jennifer by the arm.

Dwayne had to resist the urge to jump out of the car with every ounce of self-control. He was beyond mad when the truth dawned on him that Bernice was indeed one of the bad guys and involved in a conspiracy to kill Jennifer.

Frank pointed with his arm at Jennifer. "Here she is. Now, let Rhea go."

"Not until she is safe in that car," Marco yapped back, gesturing with his head towards his vehicle. "You've already tried to kill her once. The moment I let Rhea go, John will shoot. I know this game, Frank. Vanessa goes first."

Frank ordered Bernice to remove the cuffs from Vanessa's wrists, then he shoved her with so much force into Marco's direction that she stumbled. She jumped up and ran as fast as she could to Marco.

Frank began to explain himself. "You know, back then, when we took her onto John's yacht, it was Bernice's idea to make her suffer. I wanted to sedate her before she was thrown into the ocean, so that she could pass out and wouldn't feel anything when she drowned, but Bernice said no."

"And today, Frank? Who brought her here today?" Marco was fully aware of and prepared for the definite shootout the moment both women were free.

He did not take his eyes from Frank while he commanded Vanessa to get into his car.

"I can't leave you here," she objected. "You are coming with me or I am staying."

"We have discussed situations like this one, numerous times in the past. I'll be right behind you, I promise. Now, go!"

John raised his weapon again and aimed it at her.

Marco lifted his chin. "Frank, if anything happens to Vanessa, I won't even think twice about shooting Rhea! And her blood will be on your hands. Tell John to lower his weapon! My patience is just about done."

Nobody paid any attention to Rhea's desperate cry.

"Dammit, John, put it down! Do you want my wife to die too?" He seemed quite on edge with Rhea there. It obviously never once crossed his mind that

Marco would bring her along. He glared back at Marco. "I wouldn't have harmed her. I thought that since she cannot remember anything, I will keep your secret and spare her life. She is kind of family after all. But yesterday, when she regained her memory, and remembered Buddy, I panicked. I had no other choice but to call John and tell him everything. We could have settled everything today in private, but no, you had to involve Rhea!"

Marco shook his head, fed up with Frank's pathetic excuses, then instructed Vanessa to go to his vehicle instantly.

She ran as fast as she could, jumped in and slammed the door shut; and they sped away.

As they left the parking lot, police cars came rushing past them. The vehicles had not even come to a complete standstill when some of the police officers jumped out and started shooting.

Heavy gunfire erupted.

In the crossfire a bullet hit Rhea and she collapsed.

Frank's painfilled scream could be heard above the blazing gunfire. "No! Rhea! My baby! NO!"

A police official tackled and forced him to the ground when he abandoned his weapon to get to her.

"No! Leave me! I have to get to my wife!" He struggled and pled to no avail. His hands were cuffed quickly and the official kept him firmly on the ground.

John dropped his weapon as soon as Bernice and Frank were both caught and cuffed. During the mini combat, he had wounded some of his colleagues too. He sounded pleased. "Thank you, everybody. I am Lieutenant Colonel John Hall, in charge of the undercover investigation regarding the smuggling of children. I have arranged this situation in order to arrest these people, who I have learned are the heads of the operation, and also the link to the East. Good job, Comrades."

"Sorry, sir," Captain Brett swung John's arms behind his back, "we have strict orders from rank higher than yours to bring you in too. Colonel Payne said we must arrest each and every one at the scene, *she* will decide who gets to go free." Then he recited his Miranda rights.

Jennifer ducked down when the first police vehicle passed them. Her heart was in her throat. If they saw her, it would be over and done. She stayed hiding for a few minutes, then sat up again. Relieved that they were not being chased down.

"Don't you understand the meaning of going fast? Go!" She glared at the driver, who was going way too slow for her liking.

"Are you okay? Did they hurt you?" He stepped on the pedal to go even faster.

"Dwayne? Is that you?" She was stunned to recognize his voice. She did not expect *him* to be Marco's backup.

"Yes, it's me. Are you hurt?"

"Nothing I can't handle. I've definitely survived worse." She would much rather not tell him what John and Bernice did to her while they were waiting for Marco to show up. She had to be honest; she was quite confused earlier when Frank was apparently in no hurry to reach their destination. Which left them with only ten to fifteen minutes to torture her; perhaps he expected Marco to arrive later than he did.

She turned her head and stared into the distance. They had left the scene in such a hurry that she had absolutely no idea if Marco had made it out safely before the action started.

13

The address Dwayne had punched into his phone's GPS led them to an empty house in a secluded area.

"Wait here, let me go and check it out," he said to her.

He quickly opened the garage door manually, entered and looked around cautiously. The door which gave direct access to the house from the garage, was open. Then he went back, got into the car, parked it in the garage and closed it from the inside. They entered the empty house through the entrance from the garage.

Only then did he remove the mask and wig. "What is going on here, Jennifer? Why were those people trying to kill you? And what is Bernice's role in all of this?"

"Why are you here, Dwayne, and this after I have asked you to leave immediately?"

"Oh no, you are not going to do this now. Answer my questions, please, Jennifer." He took a stand in front of her. The expression on his face sent the message that he was not going to accept any side-tracking at all.

She sighed. "I don't know where to start."

"Start at the beginning." By now he was tired of all the evasive answers and lies. He had never been as scared in his entire life, as he was earlier when Marco fired the first shot, and he finally grasped the severity of the situation.

Her facial expression was one of guilt. "Marco and I are detectives; we do undercover operations."

"Yes, I know."

"How do you know this? Did Marco tell you?"

"It doesn't matter how I know. Please, go on."

She inhaled sharply, exhaled slowly; her face turned pale. "We were investigating human trafficking, more specifically, the smuggling of children. We were working undercover, becoming part of the operation in order to get to the big players, the main links of the operation and to shut it down completely. Bernice was one of the field leaders. I could have arrested her instantly when I discovered her involvement, but my mission was to work with her and get her to tell me who she reported to. I needed to know who the person in charge was of all Eastern trade. I finally got her to recommend me as leader and arranged a meeting with the chief."

"But, that's impossible! I have seen with my own eyes how Bernice loves those children. She is no child smuggler! Why would she do such a thing?" Although it had become clear earlier that Bernice was undeniably part of something illegal and criminal, not once did human trafficking cross his mind. This was too much to bear.

"I'm afraid it is the truth, Dwayne." She put a hand on his shoulder. She could not help but feel sorry for all the lies he had to soak up this past year, maybe even longer ... lies told by his fiancée, the one person he probably trusted the most.

"I am truly sorry, Dwayne."

He nodded his head once. His breathing was shallow.

She continued in a sad voice, "I told Marco that I was going to meet the chief, but he did not believe me. So, I went alone. When I arrived, it turned out that the person in charge, was none other than John Hall, the Lieutenant Colonel at my office. Needless to say, he recognized me, and immediately detained me. They forced me onto his yacht. He wanted to know how much I had managed to find out about his 'business'. He wanted to know if I had other partners than Marco, because he knew the two of us were working together. He demanded to know what channels we were infiltrating and all that. They kept me on that yacht for what felt like months, but in fact it was only a week. I told them nothing, no matter how brutally they assaulted me. But because I have seen them, they decided to kill me. Bernice was apparently heartbroken that I had betrayed her and suggested that I should suffer for what I had done. John commanded her to get his wife's swimwear from his cabin and forced me into them. Then they tied weights around my waist and threw me overboard."

It was almost as if she spoke from the memory, broadcasting live, with no control over what came from her mouth. She was pale and shaking uncontrollably as she revisited that scene for the millionth time since yesterday.

He listened with great attention, not interrupting. He was repulsed by the detail. Furious. Shocked. All sorts of questions ran through his mind: How could Bernice deceive him like this? How could she be involved with such revolting criminalities? How could he not have seen through her fake charm, her fake love for children?

Jennifer's voice brought him back to reality. "I did not realize that the other person was actually Frank. He was introduced to me as Buddy Butler, but I had failed to noticed that he was in disguise. I am convinced, had I seen Frank that week on the yacht, I would surely have recognized him when Marco dropped me off there. Like I did with John and Bernice. ... I only realized I was left in the care of my archenemy when he took me away this morning."

"But ... he was still at home when you left. He said someone else came to pick you up."

"No, he woke me up very early and asked if I could help him with something in the garage. At first, I was a little surprised by his request, but I was always up early, helping him with work on the farm. So, I followed him out. When we entered the garage, however, he grabbed me, tied me up and made sure that there was no way I could make a sound, or cry for help. Then he tossed me into the trunk of his car, and left me there for a good couple of hours, before finally coming back and taking off. After a while, he stopped, we were quite a distance from the farm by then. He let me out of the trunk, untied me, ripped the duct tape from my mouth and pushed me into the passenger seat. Threatening to shoot me on the spot if I even thought about running away or screaming for help while he walked around the car to get behind the steering wheel again. At that stage, I had absolutely no idea why Frank would kidnap me at all. Then he transformed into Buddy in front of my eyes, as he put on his disguise. That's when I knew I was in much bigger danger than I originally thought." The tears were touching her voice and eyes, but she tried her best to keep them at bay. Because she knew, once they started rolling, there would be no stopping them.

He frowned as he processed her words. "Does this mean you were on the farm the entire time, until Frank eventually left at nine, telling us he was going to town?"

"Yes."

He stepped forward and put his arms around her. "I am so sorry, Jennifer. If only I knew, I would have fetched you from the car immediately and confronted Frank myself." He knew his words of comfort would do nothing to set her at ease, but he had to try at least. Anger, sorrow and rage overwhelmed him all at once. He pulled her even tighter to his chest, but almost immediately loosened his grip again.

She stood motionless in his arms, tears rolling down her cheeks. She could not explain why she had become so emotional lately. She had worked among hardened criminals for years already, without ever being affected like this. In the past, she had always managed to distance herself and focus on the objectives of the case. Why was this case so different? Even the torture should not have affected her like this – the academy did way worse things to her in her preparation to become an undercover detective.

"I am sorry." She whispered into his chest.

"Sorry for what?"

"I don't know what has gotten into me lately. I am never this emotional."

He replied in a tender voice. "Don't be sorry for being human."

"I have been trained not to give in under pressure, not to become attached, not to talk about my operations and not to follow orders blindly. Today alone, I have failed in all of those regards. And by doing so, I have put both your and Marco's life in danger. So, I have to apologize."

He released his embrace entirely, put his hands on her shoulders as he pushed her an arm length away so he could look her in the eye. "There is nothing wrong with what you did today. Your life was in great danger; you did what you had to do to survive. You did not give in under the pressure; you kept a clear mind the entire time. Even now, I can see you are in tremendous pain, but you don't say a word about it."

She opened her mouth, but he silenced her. "Don't even try to deny it. I felt how your body cramped from discomfort when I hugged you. You've been trying to keep your emotions and the fact that you were tortured from me this entire time. Any other person would have snapped hours ago. But not you. You are the strongest person I have ever met."

"I don't think so."

"Believe me." He stroked her hair, and gazed into her eyes as her head tilted backwards.

The door flew open and Marco entered.

The first thing he witnessed, was them staring into each other's eyes and Dwayne gently stroking her hair.

She let go of Dwayne and ran into Marco's arms.

He was caught off guard by this, but he automatically put his arms around her waist. He shut his eyes to absorb the moment completely, so he could hold onto it when he had to leave later. This was the first time she had ever been in his arms, so even if this was purely out of gratitude, he prolonged the moment by pulling her tighter against his chest.

The pain shot through her body, but she concentrated hard not to move a muscle. He did not need to know too; it was bad enough that she could not hide it from Dwayne. So, she absorbed the pain by biting on her teeth.

"Thank you, Marco," she said after a few seconds in a hoarse voice; her arms wrapped around his neck. "How did you know where to find me? How did you know it was Frank all along?"

"It doesn't matter anymore. All that matters, is that I did." Chills ran down his spine as he imagined what could have happened, had he failed to save her from those monsters in whose hands she had fallen for a second time.

He touched her forehead with his and closed his eyes again. Then it hit him that since her memory had returned, she probably also recalled that their marriage was fake, only part of their cover. A burning feeling shot through his heart when he realized yet again that she had never reached the point where she had fallen in love with him, like he did with her. It hurt so much, it almost felt unreal. For her, it was all about the case, and nothing more.

"How did you get here?" Dwayne interrupted their intimate moment.

She stepped out of Marco's arms.

Marco glared at him. "Sometimes it is best not to know everything, Dwayne."

His eyes moved from Dwayne to Jennifer. "We don't have much time. We have to act fast. My house is probably already surrounded; it won't take long before they come here."

The house he referred to, was actually a rental to protect their private lives from their enemy whom they necessarily had to invite and entertain as teachers; to give authenticity to their cover. They had to lure them in; gain their trust. Then, when everything was supposed to be over and done, and the criminals realized that they were actually undercover detectives, they would not be able to get to them. The plan was to move out of the rental, and back into their own properties as soon as the case was closed. But since he was caught off guard by the sudden change of events, he did not have the time to move out, or to retrieve the keys to his private property from Colonel Payne, who took it when they started working this case. He didn't even think about getting his keys back when he was demoted, because he believed he would be back on the case as soon as he managed to expose Hall.

"I promise, this is the last time I will ever change your name, Adelaide. Here is your final identity: Madeline Brooks..."

"Wait a second," Dwayne cut him short. "Adelaide?"

"Yes, there is no point in keeping it secret any longer. That is actually her real name, it was changed to Vanessa merely a year and a half ago, when we were assigned to our last case."

His jaw dropped and he gazed at Jennifer, or Adelaide, or is it Madeline – he can't keep up with all her name changes.

"So, you *are* Adelaide." Then she actually did remember her real name when she was still suffering from amnesia. He felt guilty for not believing her at the time.

Her smile only touched her lips, it did not reach her eyes which were filled with sadness.

"Dwayne," Marco waited until Dwayne made eye contact with him before continuing, "will you take her as far away from here as you possibly can, please?"

"Uhm, of course, where ..."

"Good. So, you will marry her right away?"

Dwayne glanced at her, then gazed back at Marco. "I will, but what ..?"

"Please excuse us for a few minutes, Adelaide, I have to talk to him in private. Come, Dwayne."

"Of course," she responded, frowning.

They exited.

As Marco led the way to one of the rooms, he recalled her incredible emotional struggle with this case before her disappearance. She had a high success rate in priority cases already, especially involving smuggling. That was why she was selected for this case. He could not understand why it was bothering her so much. Her success rate was regarded as one of the best in the Force. Her methods were very efficient, but in this last case, it seemed like she was really struggling not to drop the ball. She had even done something unheard of for her: she had asked to be removed from the case. Repeatedly. One night he had found her crying in her bed. He went and sat at her side, and comforted her. This quickly became a daily routine before he would go to his room.

He remembered asking her why she was crying. She told him how she was haunted by every little child whose life she had ruined. How she heard their voices, saw their faces as they asked her, in her mind, why she betrayed them, why she killed them. She said she could hear the parents crying as they realized their children were never coming home again. "And it's all because of me!"

In an attempt to help her cope with the situation, he reminded her that those children were already ordered, if she did not take them, Bernice would have done it anyway.

"That is so cruel." She had replied, sobbing. "How can anybody do that to little innocent children – buy and sell them like goods, and not even feel guilty about it? Now I am one of them. I have become an animal, a monster. I don't care if I did it for a good reason! I bet, if you ask those little kids, they won't agree. They get injected with so many drugs that they don't even know who they are. You should see them, Marco," she had looked at him as if she thought he did not know. "They can't even talk, or walk, they are in so much pain, but they can't do anything about it!"

"So, you think that those drugs you helped smuggle on your previous case, did not also ruin lives? You don't think countless parents lost their children to drugs too? Or relationships crumbled; people going into debt or turn to theft, only to buy those drugs; or overdose and die, leaving their loved ones in agony?" He knew his words were harsh and did not help much with her emotional struggle, but he thought she needed to hear it. In his eyes, smuggling drugs and smuggling children were equally evil and had the same destructive consequences. He could not understand why she did not see it like that too, and why she had such a big issue all of a sudden. "Because of you, the greatest drug dealers and distributors in this country have been taken down. Look at the impact it had on the presence of drugs lately. This will be the same, think of how many lives we'll save by doing this, instead of focusing on the collateral damage."

Those few seconds before she responded, only staring at him, had given him chills all over his body. The expression on her face, and how it made him feel, was beyond explanation.

Her voice sounded strangely cold when she finally said that smuggling drugs and smuggling children were nothing alike. When she smuggled drugs, the product was not a human being, she did not have to look into the parcel's eyes and lie to its face before giving it to dangerous people who have no conscience whatsoever.

While they were having that conversation, he had become aware of a strange sensation in his heart, one he had never felt before. As days went by and he had time to think about it, he realized that he had feelings for her, but he wasn't sure if it was love. The feeling only grew stronger. Gradually, he was willing to do more and more for her, to the point where he would do anything for her.

In that last week before she disappeared, something changed. She started working ferociously; he even applauded her on her new found enthusiasm. She responded that she only wanted this mission to be over and done, so that she could hand in her resignation. What shocked him even more, however, was when she added that everything they were doing, was not worth anything at all. She claimed that they would not even make a dent in the market, because it was so intricate that even if they did manage to cut off the main link in Durban, it would take the human traffickers less than a week to be back on speed.

She was in tears when she continued, "The only thing we are doing, is destroying ourselves. This operation has failed."

It was because of this conversation that he was suspicious later when she said that she was about to meet the leader. In his mind, she had gotten so desperate to end this investigation that she was starting to lose focus, and imagining herself all sorts of things. ... If only he had taken her seriously.

"You wanted to talk?" Dwayne's voice jolted him back to the present.

It took him a moment to get his thoughts together again. "Yes. ... I'm sure you have heard by now what we are doing for a living."

Dwayne nodded.

"The case we were working on, has gone horribly wrong. The people we were investigating, found out she was working undercover, consequently they kidnapped her. They tried to get her to talk and give info about the investigation, but they underestimated her. So, they threw her into the ocean. You were just in time to save her life, but her brain got a little damaged and her memory got locked up."

He stopped talking, thinking how different it could have been if he had gone with her. He could have saved her. Extraction of high value targets from dangerous situations, was another one of his specialties, besides leading hardened criminals into carefully set traps.

Dwayne was becoming somewhat impatient. He knew all this information already. Couldn't Marco skip to the part that required them to be alone? Besides, what was Marco thinking suggesting them getting married, how exactly would that keep her safe?

Marco sighed, then continued, "I was supposed to kill her, because she had lost her memory. But since I didn't; and because my superiors know about it now, I am going to pay for it with my own life. No less than three snipers will already have received their orders, and they will definitely be in position by now. The moment I set foot at my house; I am gone. Poof.

Never existed. It's the way the boss created the system. No room for error."

"Then why don't you leave with her? Change your identity, and get out while you can."

"No, that will only result in both of us dying. I'll give my life today to buy her some time to get out alive." He sounded dead already.

"That's ridiculous."

Marco shook his head. He was so certain that he was on top of the situation, two steps ahead of Payne and John. He was sure he would get her out of the country before anyone could discover she was alive. His plan was to tell her he loved her when he put her on the plane and asked her to wait for him. Then he would have waited a few months, even a year, if necessary, to resign and reunite with her. But now, he felt miles behind. He was so busy working on Adelaide's escape plan, he didn't once think about his own. He did not create any new identity or escape route for himself. She got her memory back at the worst time ever. After the bombs of truth dropped this morning, his only purpose was not to die in the inevitable shootout, but to get her out safely first.

He tried hard to focus on the matter at hand. "Dwayne, the moment I decided not to kill her, I had sealed my fate. I have prepared myself for what is about to come. I cannot leave here alive. Now I need you to keep her safe. It would have been even better if you could have taken her out of the country. Please, don't let this sacrifice I am about to make for her to live, be in vain. Promise me!"

"Yes, yes, I promise," he replied at Marco's sudden change of tone. His thoughts dwelled for a moment, then he said, "My sister and her husband are constantly pleading with me to move to America with them. He runs a business there and wants me to join him. I had declined until now, because I have my own thriving business here, but it might be time to reconsider. I'll phone him tonight and ask him to start with the necessary arrangements immediately. I'll see to it that Adelaide gets out of the country as soon as possible."

It appeared as though a ton of weight had instantly fallen from Marco's exhausted shoulders. "Thank you."

"You know, it was truly a coincidence that my Cruiser broke down in front of the farm where you hid her."

"I do not believe in coincidences, Dwayne. It is definitely no coincidence that your paths keep crossing each time when she is in danger. There is a reason you keep finding her when she needs someone the most. It would be the wise thing to do, for me, to leave her in the care of her guardian angel."

They looked each other in the eye for a while, their minds finally merged.

A frown appeared on Dwayne's forehead when the thought crossed his mind that there was no greater testimony of one's love than to die for someone.

"Does she know how you feel about her? Does she know what you are about to do?" He waited for Marco to answer, but he only stared at him with a lost expression on his face.

"Does she know you love her?" he rephrased.

"We have never loved each other. Not in that way. Our marriage was a pretense. We only lived together not to blow our cover, but when we were behind locked doors, we barely even spoke, barely even saw each other. You understand what I am saying, Dwayne?" He paused, then continued, "I would have done the same for any of my other colleagues."

He tried his best to convince Dwayne differently, but Dwayne knew instinctively Marco did not see her as just another colleague, and that he loved her dearly.

All of a sudden, Dwayne felt sorry for him. While he did not quite comprehend everything, and he knew he was no Knight in Shining Armer who could grand her better protection than Marco could, he clearly understood that Marco was not in control of the situation anymore.

"Come," said Marco, "we have to hurry."

They entered the empty living room where Adelaide waited for them, then Marco spoke, "I have to go home now."

She gave a step closer to him. "You can't go home! You said yourself what waits there."

"No Adelaide, I've spoken to Colonel Payne and told her that John is the culprit and the man we have been hunting all this time. She believes me. She trusts me. She's the one who sent backup earlier today. She doesn't know you are alive, and if she does, I will tell her that you have regained your memory, and you hold no threat to anyone."

"But you said your house is probably surrounded already. And we both know that is the truth."

He took a deep breath and exhaled slowly but cautiously so she wouldn't notice his nervousness. In his panic earlier he had voiced his fear openly. He knew she would not leave with Dwayne if she was not convinced that he would be safe.

"Listen, Adelaide, when I arrived, I was distracted by the shootout and spoke without thinking. Now that I have calmed down and the paranoia has settled, I am convinced my house is not surrounded. Colonel Payne doesn't know anything, so she would not have sent the snipers. I promise you; nothing will happen to me when I get home. Your life is the one in danger if you stay here. I need you to go with Dwayne and start a new life, free from this. You said you wanted to resign when this case is over, remember? There are only three people who know who Madeline Brooks really is, and we are all present in this room. If Dwayne can get you abroad as quickly as possible, you will never be found."

She narrowed her eyes as she looked at him, then said, "All right, Marco, I'll follow your orders. Come, Dwayne, let's go."

"Take the car you came with." He turned towards Dwayne, "You have the key."

"Will it be safe? The police will know it is your vehicle if they run the numberplate."

"You'll be safe. I have registered that vehicle in Madeline Brooks' name last week."

"Thanks, Marco. Then let's go now." She left with Dwayne, off to their new life.

"Where to?" he asked when they hit the highway.

"Anywhere but your house."

He jerked his head into her direction, "Why can't we go to my house?"

"Because it might be under surveillance too."

"Why? I am not involved in the case."

"You drove the escape vehicle with me inside, so according to them, you are involved."

His heart sank to his feet, but then he relaxed. "I was wearing a disguise when we went to get you. Who would even know that I was there?"

"Rhea knows, and although she might be arrested with the others, nothing stops her from mentioning you, and having Colonel Payne onto us in no time," she responded, oblivious to the fact that Rhea had passed away on the scene earlier.

He could hear the nervousness in her voice and decided to take caution and not go home.

She turned her head and stared out of the window, into the distance. She knew Marco had lied earlier. His house would definitely be surrounded. She knew him very well; they had lived together for almost a year and a half after all. She could tell he was terrified of going home, and that he was only pretending to be calm. While she could not understand why he opted not to leave with them, she decided not to push him. He was a grown man who made his own decisions.

His strange behavior spurred another fearful thought, though, that Payne actually knew she was alive. The more she thought about it, the more convinced she was that that was indeed true. Even if Payne did not know about it beforehand, the officers would tell her, if anyone of them had seen her fleeing from the scene by any chance. And if none of them had seen anything, the mere fact that Marco did not go to the station directly after the shootout, would surely have created lots of suspicion. Not to mention Rhea, Frank, Bernice and John all knew about her escape, and none of them would think twice about selling her out.

Then she wondered if perhaps Marco had his own escape plan and that he was not going home after all. He probably had planed to run too. The thought that he might actually be safe, gave her some sense of relief.

Dwayne's voice jerked her back to the present. "Do you think Marco was serious about us getting married straight away?"

"Yes."

"In that case, we won't have the time to arrange a normal wedding ..."

"No."

He glanced at her. "Since our wedding is not going to be a normal one, we could just as well ask the pastor in the town wherever we end up tonight, to marry us. If it is okay with you? And if we have to wait for the pastor, we can stay for a day or two. We can ask some of the local people to be the witnesses."

She nodded, unhappy to be in this situation. Yet another fake marriage...

Hours later they arrived at a small town and decided to spend the night there. After checking in at a motel, they went strolling through the streets to stretch their legs.

"Jennifer ... I mean Madeline?"

"Yes?"

"I'm so sorry for everything Bernice put you through." He was struggling to accept the fact that Bernice was a child selling monster. But even he could not argue away the evidence. She was present when Madeline was tortured and almost killed both times. He even heard Frank said it was Bernice who insisted she suffered a slow death.

"Thanks, Dwayne." She hesitated for a moment, then decided that if they were going to trust each other, there should be no secrets between them.

So, she told him everything about her last mission and the time on the yacht with Bernice, Frank and John. Shivers ran down her spine as she relived that hellish week. She told him how stunned she was when she saw John, because he was not part of the team investigating that particular case. Bernice, of course, had no idea that she and John knew each other, so, she introduced her to him and Buddy. Buddy had seemed quite nervous to see her, but she now knew why. Since *he* knew she and Marco were busy with an undercover investigation, it must have hit him immediately what their mission was when he saw her. ... John, on the other hand, did not appear surprised to see her at all, almost as if he was waiting for her. A mocking smile were dancing around his lips: "Well, well, well, what have we here?" Then he told Bernice who she was and what her objective would be. He also said that there was probably a whole response team on standby, waiting for her to give the thumbs up. He sent Buddy off to go look for them. When he returned with the news that there was no backup, John had burst out laughing. She was in such sock that she completely forgot her training. By the time she had gathered herself, they were already way off shore, and she was all tied up. John was giving orders and Bernice and Buddy took turns torturing her. There was no turning back. She had abandoned all hope by the second day. She knew her life was over. It made it easier to know she would die not giving them any information. She hated herself for not listening to Marco. She should have taken him with her, or waited until he could join her. It was irresponsible to go alone.

She stopped talking to take a quick breath, then she became aware of the warm tears streaming down her cheeks; and Dwayne's hand in hers. She had no idea when she had started crying or when he took her hand.

"Madeline," he whispered.

"I'd rather not tell you everything they did to me, but I think you have a pretty good idea."

"I don't blame you. Besides, I don't think I want to know, it will drive me insane." He pulled her to a halt and then embraced her.

She allowed herself to be comforted for a brief moment.

"When they finally realized that I was not going to betray my colleagues, nor give them any information, they tied weights to my body and threw me overboard."

Her voice sounded hoarse as she told him how they kept telling her this was her last case; her last day; and then made jokes about it. How Bernice kept on yelling: "traitor!" as she was dealing blows. How she struggled to free herself from the weights and how she faintly remembered a dolphin coming to her rescue.

It took a few minutes for her to control her emotions again. "I cannot stop wondering why I could immediately recognize Bernice and John, the people who tried to kill me, but not the people I cared about? Why could I not recognize Marco or Rhea? ... Except Frank! He managed to fool me completely! He was right in front of my eyes the entire time and I failed to see it! I did not even recognize his voice. While I was living under his roof, I kept thinking how generous and caring he was, such a nice guy... I truly thought he was a good man."

He was still processing her words when she changed the topic. "Listen, I know Marco bullied you into marrying me. I am really sorry about that. I know you are engaged to Bernice, and your heart belongs to her. I do not expect you to marry me, and you are under no obligation to do so. I will leave the country on my own, Marco doesn't have to know about it, ever." She would rather go through life alone than be in another fake marriage, especially with *him*. The guilt of living with a man who loved another woman would haunt her forever. Dwayne's heart belonged to Bernice, and the disappointment in discovering that she was a criminal would eventually fade and he would make peace with it. Love conquers all.

Dwayne frowned, stunned by her words. Was she actually ignorant of the fact that Marco had laid down his life today for her? Should he enlighten her? Rather not. It would only upset her, and Marco obviously wanted to keep it from her, or else he would not have deemed it necessary to discuss the matter with him in private. It would be disrespectful to talk about it now. ... Then he remembered her telling him that his house would be surrounded too and that they could not go there. He could not help but wonder whether she was perhaps under the impression that Marco would have survived the ordeal.

He chose his words carefully. "Do you think the police would have arrested Marco when he got home earlier today?"

"No, definitely not. They would have shot him the instant he set foot in his yard."

Rather upset by the careless tone in her voice, he gasped. "And that doesn't bother you?"

A meaningful smile appeared on her face. "No, because they would have waited for him in vain. There is no way Marco would have returned home today. They will never find him; he is a genius in this regard. I am convinced he had his own escape plan ready, which was set in motion when he left that house where we all were earlier."

"What makes you so sure about that?" Sadly, he knew the truth. Marco was not on top of his game, the pressure had taken its toll, and he made it crystal clear that he was about to sacrifice himself to buy her time to get out alive.

"I have a feeling. I know him well. The way he tried to get you and me married so quickly, and the way he seemed so eager to leave, made me suspicious. ... Listen, no one can force you to marry me."

"Who says I am going to do it because I am forced?"

Before she could even respond, his hands folded around her wrists and he continued, "If you only waited for three seconds after you kissed me yesterday, before you chased me away, you would have known that I love you, more than anything or anyone else in this world."

"But ... what about Bernice? You're engaged."

He slid his hands from her wrists all the way up to her shoulders. "No, Madeline, I ended that engagement a week ago since our relationship was going nowhere anyway. We had not spoken to each other for ages, so I went to her house and called off this so-called engagement. In fact, I was actually returning from Bernice when my Cruiser broke down and I found you at Frank and Rhea's place. I could not believe my eyes when I saw you there, Jenif... I mean Madeline. If you can only know how much I had thought about you after I left you at Marco's house. I did not want to intrude and create an uncomfortable situation in your marriage, that is why I did not maintain contact, or visited. But I thought and worried about you, every single day. I thought about what you told me on the yacht; and what you said about Bernice. The impact you had on my life in those few short-lived days, was so vast, it changed my life, and it changed who I am. I started looking at the world and at people differently. I soon realized that what I felt for Bernice was not true love. To be honest, it was not love at all. Besides, the way she treated me, and made me feel, was not what I had envisioned for my future. But you, you opened my eyes. So, I took two weeks' vacation, not only to break off my engagement with Bernice, but I desperately wanted to see you again. I wanted to know how you were doing, and I was not even going to let Marco stop me. I was so disappointed when he claimed to have never met you, and that you did not live there. This past week on the farm with you, has been the best week of my life. And it dawned on me that you had completely stolen my heart on that day when you accused me of trying to kill you, and banged with your fists on my chest with everything you had. I failed to realize it before, but I love you. Madeline, I love everything about you."

She put her hands on his chest. "I love you too, Dwayne."

Hearing her say those words, wiped out his fear that she might not feel the same as he did. Waves of relief exploded through his body. He was so afraid that, like Marco, she too might have developed feelings for him in the course of their fake marriage. After all, they did live in the same house for quite some time, and got to know each other pretty well. They had to look out for one another, be there for each other when life happened, and most likely shared secrets, which could have easily sprouted into love.

He pulled her closer for a kiss. Her arms circled around his neck and she kissed him back.

"So, you are not marrying me simply because Marco told you too?"

"No, Dwayne, I agreed to marry you because I love you and want to lie in your arms every single night. I want to listen to your voice as we fall asleep. I want to spend the rest of my life being with you."

He pulled her even closer, holding her tighter and kissed her again. Then they walked hand in hand back to their accommodation.

"Remember, not even Pedro can know that Madeline and Vanessa are the same person."

"Why not?" He responded without thinking, then realized why, and answered himself, "Of course. Bernice knows that he met you and might mention his name to the police. They might question him, and he might lead them to us."

She felt miserably guilty, because he had to give up all his friends, his beloved career and his country for her. "I am sorry about all of this, Dwayne," she whispered.

He glanced at her. "I've been in need of a good long break away for a while now. As soon as we are married, I'll call Pedro and tell him I met someone by the name of Madeline and we fell head over heels in love, so much so that we decided to get married straight away. I'll tell him that we will be away on honeymoon for at least two months and that he can take charge of the show in the meantime."

"I only wish you didn't have to give up your show, it is heartbreaking. I've seen how much you love it."

He stared into the distance. Marco had warned him the day of their first meeting that his life would change irrevocably if he did not walk away and forget he ever met Vanessa, if he did not cut all ties with her whatsoever.

He moved his shoulders slightly. "I know of a good place where we can lie low for a month or two, while my brother-in-law, Henry, gets the paperwork ready for my work visa; and your partner's visa. When everything is in place, I'll call Pedro again and tell him that you and I will be moving abroad and that the show is his. He'll get a new partner soon enough. In the meantime, I'll contact my cousin, who is an estate agent, and ask him to sell my house in private, without advertising it at all. So, if my house is under surveillance, it will not be too obvious that I'm planning to leave. Hopefully the spies will get tired of watching my house within the next few days. If all goes well, we'll be settling in America soon."

"Thank you, Dwayne, I appreciate the sacrifices you're making specially for me."

He smiled and said in a playful tone, "I'll do anything for you, as long as you are by my side ... my little mermaid."

Her heartbeat started racing as she gazed into his eyes that burned with desire. This was the first night they were truly alone. She whispered his name and moved in to receive yet another kiss.

14

Surprised at making it all the way to his front door, Marco entered the house and did not bother to close the door behind him. He had been certain he would not even be able to take as much as two steps from his car before he met his fate. Since he knew what awaited him, he deliberately did not scrutinize the area around his house when he approached. He convinced himself that it was best not to know where they were hiding.

In his core, he could feel something was not quite right. Why was he still alive? This made him nervous; he walked slowly through the entrance area. No sound came from anywhere, only an almost terrifying silence filled the space.

When he passed the door leading to the lounge, he noticed Colonel Payne on one of the couches. He had actually expected to find someone in the house, because there was nobody outside waiting to take his life, nevertheless he was startled by her presence. Without saying anything, he continued walking, even tenser than before, peering cautiously into each room. He found no one else hiding anywhere. His heart was in his throat. It was well-known that Colonel

Payne never executed anyone personally, ever! She always hired someone to do her dirty work.

"Satisfied, Vincent?" She spoke when he entered the lounge and sank down on the couch opposite her in silence.

He only nodded, completely uncomfortable in his own house – a feeling no one should ever have.

"You betrayed me," she said in her calm, threatening voice.

His mouth became dry and his heart pounded violently against his ribcage. Just because he knew he was going to die, did not make it less frightening, and her dragging it out, was even worse.

Payne was known for never making exceptions to her rules, she also never negotiated with those beneath her. Especially not if she believed that person to be a traitor.

After an awkward silence, he replied, "I have not betrayed you, Colonel."

"Where is Vanessa?" The tone in her voice and the expression in her eyes conveyed extreme disappointment and discontent. Her body language suggested that she knew more than she let on.

Briefly he wondered if she had perhaps already found Dwayne and Madeline, but immediately dismissed that thought. Doubt would only cause him to make mistakes; and the smallest misstep on his side would lead her to Madeline, if she was actually bluffing.

"She is dead, Colonel, as you ordered." In his opinion, this was true. Vanessa was dead to him, he will never see her again, ever! This last case ruined her, it changed her, it killed her. She had warned him numerous times that this would happen, but he didn't take her seriously. And in the end, in a way, it changed him too.

"Do you think I was born yesterday? Do you take me for a fool, Vincent? The moment you decided her life was more important than my direct order, you betrayed me." Her face became red. She moved her body slightly forward to sit on the edge of her seat.

He opened his mouth to respond, but she held up her hand, silencing him. He paid very close attention to the slightest movement of her body. He considered her behavior suspicious and utterly strange. Something about this entire business of her being here, bothered him, but he could not put his finger on it.

She narrowed her eyes while she looked at him, almost like she was between two minds. When she finally spoke, she sounded sad – something he had never witnessed.

"Why, do you think, did I make the rule that when someone loses their memory, they must die?"

"It is not my place to question your motives, Colonel." He was way past the point where he cared about her opinion of him. And he couldn't care less about her repulsive reasons as to why loyal, hardworking detectives should be killed.

"We are working with very high-profile cases, Vincent. Do you know how easy it is for traitors to pretend to have lost their memory and make all evidence of their investigation disappear? Do you know how often this happens? This puts everyone in danger. I don't want the lives of good detectives in needless danger because I didn't have the guts to eliminate a possible threat. I'd rather lose one detective who may or may not have been a double agent, than lose my entire squad because of one."

"Why would a double agent pretend to have amnesia?"

"You have a lot to learn, Vincent." She clearly tried her best to sound stern, but her voice trembled.

"Vanessa was not a double agent, Colonel, I can assure you."

Her eyes threw daggers at him, yet her voice remained calm. "I have also fallen in love once, just like you now, with a colleague, a partner. Hard as it is to believe, there was someone I trusted with my life, I would have done anything for him. We even got married and for two years my life was perfect. One day he walked into our room and said he didn't know me; he had apparently lost all of his memory. He didn't know who I was, where he worked or even who *he* was. I took him to doctors and specialists, psychologists and psychiatrists, but no one could figure out why he had lost his memory. He was not in any accident, neither had he fallen on his head. No one could help him regain his memory. Our marriage was ruined by this, we divorced and he moved out."

For the first time ever, he saw her struggling to control her emotions.

She closed her eyes for a brief moment, then continued, "Six months later, I learned that he had never suffered from amnesia at all. Apparently, he didn't love me anymore, and about a week after our separation, he married someone else – the very person we were investigating for major global fraud. While we were still married, and he pretended to have amnesia, I showed him photos of us, and evidence of our cases. He went behind my back and tampered with the evidence and destroyed crucial information we needed to take her down. Two of our team members got killed in the process – but the two of *them* got away, we had nothing to take her down with anymore. It all went flying out the window, and they walked home singing, with a brand-new pay check. Hiding behind amnesia is a far too easy way to get free from your duties and liabilities. I won't allow anyone else to be the victim of that again. It is way too easy to use that as an excuse. Unlike any other illness, amnesia is undetectable and untreatable, it is a 'get out of jail free' card. Well, not on my watch; not ever again."

He could hardly believe that she had told him her life's story. That was unheard of; he was so caught off guard, he almost forgot why she was here to begin with. Initially, when she started telling him this, he thought she was only trying to manipulate him, but not anymore. "I am sorry you had to go through such a terrible thing. No person should have to endure that."

On the one hand, he felt a little bit sorry for her. On the other hand, he was angry at her for letting her personal bad experience ruin the lives of all those who worked under her command and might indeed suffer from memory loss, like Adelaide did. And now *he* had lost the only woman he ever loved; she was out of his reach, forever. And it was all *her* fault! The absolute misuse of her power to punish everyone else for her husband's sins, was a crime in itself.

She regained her composure. "Vincent, the only reason you are still alive, is because you have showed me that there is a small piece of loyalty left in you. Because you persistently asked me to investigate Hall, despite all my resistance, you demonstrated that you care for the truth and the future of this department. If not for that, I would not even have dispatched backup this morning when you requested it. I am going to make an exception here today. You have earned yourself a second chance to prove to me that I have your complete loyalty. Do not betray me again. Next time I will not be so generous."

"Thank you, Colonel."

A nod was all he received, then she said, "As of tomorrow, you will take Hall's place as Lieutenant Colonel. Congratulations."

He gaped at her in total surprise. Flabbergasted. He was so surprised; he did not even get up when she did.

She headed towards the door, but before she exited the lounge completely, she turned around, smiled and asked in a sweet voice, "So, where is she?"

He instantly knew this question was not as innocent as she pretended it to be. His heartrate got out of control as he asked himself whether this meeting was anything it seemed to be at all. His entire body shivered uncontrollably and he started to panic. Fear set in. He'd let his guard down! The only reason she had told him her story was for him to understand why she was not going to withdraw her order to have Vanessa killed. If he told her now that Vanessa had regained her memory and posed no threat to the team whatsoever, it would be a confession that she was still alive and that he had lied to her face a few moments ago. Even if she claimed to know about Vanessa being alive, there was the slight possibility that she didn't actually know for sure and that she was only bluffing.

Without answering immediately, he got up slowly. Nothing in his composure gave away how petrified he was really. *Keep it together, keep it together,* he kept on repeating in his mind.

His eyes did not waver nor did he look away from her, "I've told you; Vanessa is dead."

His heart almost stopped beating when she threw her head back and laughed out loud. She clearly did not believe him at all. In fact, her body language screamed out that he should not think he had outsmarted her.

But that was exactly what he thought.

He was not an undercover detective for nothing. She would never hear the truth from his mouth as long as he lived. His job required him to play any role to perfection, until he achieved the desired results, even if it took years. His new part to play from now on would be that of 'The man who killed Vanessa', simple as that. It would not even be difficult to pretend that she no longer lived anyway, because it was true to some extent. He was prepared to die for her today, torture would make no difference. He would never betray his love.

He despised Colonel Payne. He had no idea if he would be able to work by her side without her noticing his resentment at some point in time. Then the perfect solution popped up in his mind. He would keep his eyes open for the first opportunity to be transferred.

For a brief moment he felt relieved because he had created yet another identity for Adelaide when she was hiding at Frank's. Madeline. If it was not for that stroke of instinct, she would have been found and killed within days, if not hours. Payne had all the resources at her disposal to trace Vanessa effortlessly. Most likely, she had also heard by now that her 'new' identity was Jennifer, since John would have gladly shared that piece of information already. It was probably he who told her Vanessa was still alive too. Hopefully she was mistrusting that scumbag by now so much so that she did not believe a word he said. And that she was only fishing to see if *he* would confirm the speculations. But she had made a huge mistake if she thought he would ever admit that Vanessa was alive and where she was hiding, not that he knew where she was at all. But even if he did, he would not tell.

The paranoia sneaked back into his heart when he wondered yet again whether Payne knew more than she let on, or whether she was only bluffing. Did she in fact have no idea where Vanessa was, and *this* was her way to get him talking, by creating the illusion that she actually knew?

If there was ever a moment in time in which he was glad that he forced Adelaide onto Dwayne and insisted they fled the country, that moment was now. All he could hope for, was that they got to America safely before Payne found them. Payne was most definitely going to search for her – and when she searched, she left no stone unturned.

She kept eye contact with him, eyebrows raised, an evil smile touching her lips. Then she waved goodbye and left.

He waited until he was absolutely certain that she was gone before he went to the front door and grabbed hold of it. He was about to shut it, when he paused to listen to the birds chirping. It's funny how the small things became significant when you so nearly escaped death. His eyes moved downwards from the tree branches and he observed the bright colors of the flowers in the garden. Their sweet soft aroma filled the air, he could not even remember when last he smelled it.

A sigh of relief escaped his mouth, these past few hours were extremely tense. He stepped outside to admire the blue sky too, then bent forward to let the green grass slide through his fingers, it was still soft from the rain the other day. Slowly he straightened again and closed his eyes, appreciating the peace of nature.

At that exact moment, three snipers fired their muffled shots simultaneously.

Dear Reader

We hope you enjoyed reading our book and found it engaging. Your feedback is very important to us and to future readers.

We would greatly appreciate it if you could take a few moments to write a review on Amazon. Your opinion helps others make informed decisions and helps us better understand what our readers value.

Thank you very much for your support!

Kind regards

The Malherbe Team